TOKYO

TOKYO

Michael Mejia

FC2

TUSCALOOSA

FC2 is an imprint of The University of Alabama Press
Inquiries about reproducing material from this work should be addressed to the
University of Alabama Press

Book Design: Publications Unit, Department of English, Illinois State University;
    Director: Steve Halle, Production Assistant: Sanam Shahmiri
Cover image: YAMAGUCHI Akira, *Raigo*, oil, sumi (Japanese ink) on canvas,
    181.8 x 227.3 cm; photo by MIYAJIMA Kei, courtesy of Mizuma Art Gallery
Cover Design: Lou Robinson
Typeface: Avenir Next Condensed and Baskerville

Library of Congress Cataloging-in-Publication

Names: Mejia, Michael, 1968- author.
Title: Tokyo / Michael Mejia.
Description: Tuscaloosa : FC2, [2018]
Identifiers: LCCN 2017045231 (print) | LCCN 2017049872 (ebook) | ISBN
  9781573668774 (ebook) | ISBN 9781573660662 (softcover)
Subjects: LCSH: Interpersonal relations—Fiction. | Tokyo (Japan)—Fiction.
Classification: LCC PS3613.E444 (ebook) | LCC PS3613.E444 T65 2018 (print) |
  DDC 813/.6—dc23
LC record available at https://lccn.loc.gov/2017045231

This project is supported in part by an award from the National Endowment for
the Arts.

ART WORKS.

**National
Endowment
for the Arts**
arts.gov

For my singular M—

CONTENTS

TOKYO

I.

Report of Ito Sadohara,
Head of Tuna, Uokai, Ltd.,
to the Ministry of Commerce,
Regarding Recent Events
in the Domestic Fishing Industry

Minister:

In accordance with my initial offer to do so, and your office's subsequent demands, I recount here, in detail, my role in what has come to be known as "The Tuna Affair." You will find, in many instances, I have exceeded your instructions by not only narrating those actions of mine directly related to the affair—including the names of all those to whom I have spoken of this matter, as well as those who might now, at the prompting of daily media revelations, realize their unwitting role in the scandal's concealment from the general public—but also by describing parallel events that affected my personal life during the past year.

I know that much of this latter narration is highly irregular in Ministry reports. I also recognize that the recent calls from the public for the government's resignation make lengthy explanations worth somewhat less than the time and materials used to give them, and that, correspondingly, my tale should only encompass those facts necessary to determine the magnitude of my crime and to assess an appropriate punishment. Nevertheless, this rare opportunity to speak without inhibition—if only in a whisper, and in the ear of a deaf executioner—has invested me with the transcendent fearlessness required for truths such as these.

I have no hope of, nor any desire for, an opportunity to explain myself to our nation or the world at large, and I do not intend this document to serve as a justification for my thoughts or actions. I expect no degree of exoneration from the Minister or the government, no quarter in my punishment.

Finally, if I might be granted one request, I respectfully ask the Minister that, for the sake of what remains of my dignity and the dignity of those involved in the personal affairs disclosed here, this report not be reprinted or passed on to others in any form.

Submitted with the deepest humility and sincerity,
Ito Sadohara

My first encounter with what has come to be known as "The Tuna Affair" occurred in the early morning hours of 21 April this year, a Thursday, only moments after I received word that my wife, Sato, had collapsed in the frozen foods aisle of her local market and commenced labor. I was sitting at my desk, staring at a framed photograph that had not left its place in a little-used desk drawer for nearly two months, when my secretary, Miss Onazaki Hideo, entered my office for the second time that morning. The photograph, in fact, was a portrait created in a studio in America: my wife, Sato, in front of an abstract, autumnal backdrop, festive but also melancholy under soft lights, so that her pale, plum-like face glows around the thin crescent light of her smile, around her small black eyes, the sticky child's candy of her lips; Sato, a small, white softness, giftwrapped, as it were, in a knit motley of orange, pink, and green neons, the girlish hues of a lost season's boutiques. This portrait was my wife's gift to me on my thirty-sixth birthday, not quite six months after we were married, before she first saw Tokyo, before I became Head of Tuna, before our difficulties.

As of that morning, Thursday, 21 April, my wife had, in fact, been gone for several months, and I'd had no contact with her since she'd faxed me, while I was at lunch, her desire to separate. Until that morning in April, I was not aware that Sato had left Tokyo, that she had, in fact, left Japan altogether. I did not know where she was. Not until that first day of "The Tuna Affair," when the news of Sato's collapse came to me by way of a transcribed telephone message from her mother, Mrs. Daisy Kamakura, did I know that Sato had returned to her parents' home in America. San Francisco, California, to be precise. And exactly how long she had been there I still did not know.

Naturally, I found the news from America rather shocking. Not because Sato was apparently living with her mother or because she had collapsed at her local market. No, Minister, I found the news rather shocking because not until that moment, after Miss Onazaki had entered my office for the first time on the first day of "The Tuna Affair" and handed me her transcription of Mrs. Kamakura's transmission, after I had laid down my morning paper (the previous day's late edition of *Asahi*) and taken two sips of coffee (a beverage that I had begun, during my time in America, to appreciate more than tea), after my wife had been gone for months without a single attempt at communication, not until that moment, Minister, was I aware that Sato had been pregnant.

As I have stated, Sato had been gone for some time. Nearly eight months, in fact. In addition to this, the demands of my position as Uokai's Head of Tuna had limited our sexual relations prior to her departure, by which I mean that those few encounters I could recall having occurred during the second and third quarters of last year were either nonprocreative or were halted prior to any immediately apparent positive result. These were the unpleasant calculations that drifted through my mind after learning of Sato's labor.

But perhaps, I thought, I have been too hasty. Perhaps, I thought, I am simply misinterpreting Mrs. Kamakura's meaning, misreading her use of the term *labor*. Yes. Simply misreading. Repeatedly misinterpreting. In fact, had I not just been perusing an article in my morning paper about a scientific study suggesting that persistent melancholy, such as that accompanying divorce or separation or a failed attempt at self-annihilation, even melancholy existing on a deeply subconscious level, may cause chronic hallucinations and errors of distraction? (I had.) I reread the message and I reread it again and I reread it again, aloud, but each iteration seemed to further obscure the characters on the slip of paper handed to me by Miss Onazaki, to erase them one by one, until only a single pair—rendered in Miss Onazaki's impeccable, artless kanji—remained: *labor*—two sounds silencing all the rest, over-whelming syntax, inflection, meaning.

But were there not other ways the term *labor* might apply to Sato?

- physical and/or mental toil
- the pitching of a ship
- left-leaning political parties
- workers' unions
- great effort in motion
- expression of a point in minute, even unnecessary detail
- the production of goods and/or services
- production effected by difficult or forced means

Labor
- childbirth

I could not excise the possibility.

My next thought in reaction to this news was (and I am embar-rassed by it now): *bitch* (a word whose use by myself is, like my affinity for coffee, a result of my time in America; to explain my adoption of it, as opposed to numerous other, softer, Japanese epithets, I can only say that its undiluted violence gives me pleasure). That bitch was having an affair. She'd left the country with her lover, and now she'd had his child.

(At a later time, after revisiting the calculations I have already mentioned, I came to believe, I had to believe, that the cause of Sato's collapse was in fact some complication from a premature birth. There was no indication of good or ill health in Mrs. Kamakura's message, regarding mother or child. I had no choice but to assume that a birth at that particular time was wholly unexpected. Why else would a woman so close to term go into labor at a market? But at the moment I have just described, time meant nothing. Sato was gone, she was pregnant, she had fallen down in San Francisco, she was the mother of a child that could not be mine. At that moment I knew for certain that she was a faithless bitch.)

In order for the Minister to understand why I came to such a conclusion, I must explain that, directly after Sato's departure, I experienced a rather difficult period of transition back to unmarried life, which was coincident with a general downturn in profits at Uokai, Ltd. For months I faced not only the shame of having lost my wife—of sleeping and eating in a silent home, of existing without intimacy, of having to choose, when others asked about Sato's health or whereabouts, whether to lie—for a moment feeling the hopeful balm of that untruth, only to feel in the next moment my anguish redoubled—or to tell the truth and risk the equally degrading possibilities of another's display of sympathy, a distasteful and embarrassing melodrama, or respectful silence—but also, it seemed at the time, not just to me but to much of Uokai's upper management, the very likely possibility of my dismissal. Daily memos made it quite clear to every department head that, despite the tradition of lifetime employment, any drop in the productivity of our individual departments would result in global termination.

Sleepless nights, Minister. Tardiness. Comments made out of turn. Deadlines very nearly missed. Important documents creased. How many times in those first three weeks of my loneliness did I lead my department to the brink of the abyss, only blind fortune and the furious industry of Miss Onazaki holding us back?

Then came "The *Matsuo* Incident."[1] Despite the generosity of the international press in blaming the Spaniards for the violence of the final confrontation, and implicitly for the incident as a whole, I knew straightaway that the dispute had, in fact, started with me. My misreading of a minor stipulation in the most recent amendment to our trade

---

1. No doubt the Minister will recall the general details. In any case I refer him to document 30001592 in Uokai, Ltd.'s archive, *Report of Maruyama Kato, Captain of the Matsuo, on the Recent Incidents in Cadiz.*

agreement with Spain led directly to the shots fired over the freezer trawler *Matsuo*'s bow.

Nevertheless, when, in the course of his investigation, the Minister examines my company record—assuming he has not already done so—he will find no reprimand, no censure, not a single mention of "The *Matsuo* Incident." Why? I said that after Sato left me I existed without intimacy, but, as the Minister knows well from his own career, truth, like a little dog, always finds its way out into the street. At best, one can only pretend not to know it; one can kick it, treat it as the cur of rumor, and hope others will follow suit.

A few hours after the climax of "The *Matsuo* Incident," I was leaving for home and found myself in one of Uokai's normally crowded elevators alone with two colleagues whom I barely knew. They were newer, younger department heads: Hitotsume Kazunoko, a lifelong roe man whom I perceived as wholly unserious, and Kanata Hiyayaka, a rather surly fugu specialist, hired away at great expense from a company in Nagasaki, a friend of celebrities and a celebrity himself, of sorts, for whom all the younger men have great respect. At first, the three of us rode in silence, but as we descended past the fifteenth floor, Hitotsume, in the midst of a grotesque yawn, clapped me on the shoulder and shook me in an overly familiar but unthreatening manner. He leaned his head close to mine, so close I could smell the earthen scent of the tea he had drunk in an unsuccessful attempt to hide the smell of the roe he had sampled earlier that day. He said that he was very sorry for my troubles, sorry for their timing, because—I remember his words exactly, his disrespectful words—"who among us at Uokai, Ltd. suffers more at this difficult time than you, Ito, struggling with your two-headed demon." Then he patted my shoulder, again with an affectation of friendliness. He removed his hand. He smiled. Kanata said nothing, only watched the numbers changing above our heads. Hitotsume saw me look over at his friend and emitted a hissing laugh, sniggering at my speechlessness, and then goaded me with insincere exhortations to come get drunk with them. Of course, I demurred.

I went home instead and remained there for two days, knowing that no one would call for me, that I would not be dismissed for delinquency. I have been with Uokai, Ltd. for the whole of my professional life, Minister, and I have developed a deep understanding of the company's ways. In spite of the gracelessness of Hitotsume's performance, I could see that I was being given leave for the purpose of settling my personal affairs. It was my duty to honor the company's generosity.

And on the second day I did indeed regain something of myself, not slowly but all at once. I had spent nearly the entire time in bed, only a glass of water and a small bowl of sushi rice at my side, as I contemplated the nature of the demon I was supposed—by Hitotsume, in any case—to be wrestling, searching for his weaknesses, when suddenly it struck me that my demon was not one with two heads, but two demons, and, thus severed, these two, while still formidable, were rendered significantly less powerful. My initial judgment of Hitotsume had been justified after all. He was a fool, a flamboyant obfuscator.

The necessary course seemed clear: I would make one of my demons disappear. I accomplished this by choosing to believe Sato no longer felt any love for me. No doubt this will not sound like much of a solution at all, seeing as it would, and in fact did, augment the anguish and shame already plaguing me. But termination in some form, personal or professional, was clearly unavoidable. A choice had to be made. And as Sato was not present to protest my intended decision, the choice seemed quite clear.

For some weeks, however, this concession to weakness brought me even lower, to the most vile depths of self-loathing a man can know, but in proportion I applied myself ever more forcefully to the needs of my department and soon began operating with such renewed vigor that I successfully drove my self-loathing back into that dark region of forgetfulness we all possess and which allows those of us willing to ignore its existence to find ourselves capable of perfection, of nobility, perhaps even of heroism. In the month following my brief convalescence I received two commendations for my department's improved sales.

Nevertheless, I could not help but continue to love Sato, to love her enough to swear to my colleagues, in spite of their polite smiles and transparent attempts to prove me a liar by foisting their secretaries and less honorable women upon me, that I would never submit myself to a woman again. An unfortunate side effect of this oath was that, whenever she overheard me renew it, Miss Onazaki excused herself and went to the ladies' toilet to cry.

But to return to the morning of 21 April. Satisfied that I finally understood the import of Miss Onazaki's note, I pulled open the lower left-hand drawer of my desk and retrieved the aforementioned portrait of Sato, determined to smash it against the sharp corner of my desk and then to tear the photograph into a hundred pieces. I believe I can also say with a high degree of certainty that, at approximately the same moment, with the frame poised above my head, I had begun forming the idea of resigning my position, inviting Miss Onazaki out to the country for the remainder of the week, and then, at the end of a short and depraved tryst, committing seppuku.[2]

---

2. This was the only time in my life I had, or have, ever consciously considered self-annihilation to resolve a situation. As I've noted previously, during the twin crises of Sato's departure and the proximity of my dismissal by Uokai, Ltd., my inclination was toward survival. Even now, despite the massing of overwhelming armies of public and private censure against the paltry fortress of this report, I do not see any advantage to suicide.

Still—and perhaps I have placed it so to test the strength of my convictions— my uncle's wakizashi sits on display at the forward edge of my desk, facing me in my chair, resting on a fine wooden stand, where most might place a calendar or a penholder.

My uncle's name was Ito Arita, and he was one of several conspirators who orchestrated "The Mukden Incident" of 1931. By the time of his ritual suicide in 1945, shortly after the Emperor's announcement of our surrender, he had achieved the rank of captain in the Kwantung Army.

Of course, and this is where I have found my admiration to be so often misunderstood, I do not wish to imply that I condone all the actions of the Kwantung Army.

I laugh now, as I'm sure the Minister does, at such romanticisms, but as I have tried to make clear, I was enraged. Though I believed my wife to be irrevocably gone, I had never expected to gain evidence of

---

I have no passion for war. The Kwantung Army's later exploits in China were most certainly despicable and foolish. My respect is limited to the methods and results of their initial creative achievements.

Since I was a boy I have admired the aggressiveness of that force and its leaders in forging the virtually autonomous state of Manchukuo from the chaos that was China, and doing so in the face of Western resistance. This remains one of the great achievements of our nation and a feat that should, I believe, be held up to our young, often directionless employees, in all areas of Japanese industry, as an example.

Too many of them have become enraptured by the American way of life and with electronic entertainments, so that, by the time they come to Uokai, Ltd. seeking employment, they know the customs of America and of the video arcade better than those on which their nation was built, by which it survived, in which it remains unique in the world. So perverse have their tastes become that our young men no longer wish to date Japanese girls but rather seek out the blond and red-headed daughters of Western transnationals and embassies. As a result, our young women spend all their time and money trying to affect an American walk, an American laugh, an American face.

As the Minister may know, Uokai, Ltd.'s president and chief executive officer, Senkai Sakana, is a man of conservative ideals. Our corporate philosophy has remained unchanged for over one hundred years, since the company was founded by Senkai-san's great-grandfather, Senkai Inkei. The company's policies, as they are stated in the *Uokai, Ltd. Personnel Manual*, begin with the principle that a strong national economy is necessarily the first stone in the foundation of a strong nation and that, for a business to contribute successfully to the national economy, employees must be well educated regarding their place, individually as well as industrially, in their country's cultural history. To this end all employees at Uokai, Ltd., during their probationary period, are required to meet in groups, led by local priests hired specifically for this purpose, to read and study vital texts such as the *Kojiki*, the *Nihon Shoki, Konjaku Monogatari, Genji Monogatari, Heike Monogatari,* and Arizumi's three-volume contemporary history, *Nihon*. One's probation only ends following full and accurate recitations, from memory, of both the *Man'yōshū* and the *Kokinshū*, so that it will always be at Uokai, Ltd., as it was once said of "the old days," that "even the most inconsequential people were impressive."

her loss of love for me. My belief in such a loss was one I had forced upon myself out of necessity, in time accepting it as fact, a bitter remedy sweetened only by the thought that I would never procure evidence to support the *in absentia* indictment. This is what must be understood: however much maligned she was in my words, in my conscious thoughts, I had nevertheless retained a secret hope, a hope I had nearly hidden even from myself—something less than a hope, a half-formed notion without definition, without expectation—that, perhaps, Sato felt some regret about leaving me.

The message delivered by Miss Onazaki that morning destroyed this secret hope.

In that moment—one like no other in my life for its sheer brutality of thought—I seemed to experience a terrible, golden metamorphosis into something far beyond myself, something that I might have imagined with the demon face of an Ōtobide mask, a man-monster with Ōtobide's bulging eyes and flaring nostrils, mouth drawn back in inhuman surprise, fearful of his own boundless rage, his own power to destroy, powerless against the seductiveness of laying waste.

I am not a destroyer, Minister. I am not a man to advocate or carry out any wanton annihilation, but as my demon-faced torment raged through me, I admit that I was prepared to destroy, if only in effigy, not just my wife but two worlds: that of her newfound happiness and that of my regret.

But to return once more to my narrative. I had raised Sato's portrait over my head and was ready to bring it down against my desk, to shatter the faithless past in a cataclysm of glass and lacquered wood. Before I could commit this brutality, however, from somewhere near the center of the tempest of choler swirling in my temples, from out of the more placid halls of my higher faculties, came a report, like the chime of a tiny bell, a simple, calming messenger dispatched to inform me that I had struck a hollow posture, that Ōtobide's face was not mine, that I could not succeed in that role, that I could not elevate my performance to the sublime mystery of what the great Noh master Zeami termed yūgen.

I lowered my arms. I felt compelled to look once more upon the portrait before exiling it again to its abysmal drawer.

And now I have returned to the point where I began: 21 April, a Thursday. I was sitting at my desk, gazing at a photograph of my wife,[3] when Miss Onazaki entered my office for the second time that morning and announced from the doorway that someone had come to see me, a man from our wholesale tuna stall at Tsukiji, my own small fiefdom amidst the greater empire of the Tokyo Central Wholesale Market for whose regulation, accounts, and personnel I am responsible.

I could already hear my visitor's labored breathing in the outer office.[4] Without looking up, I told Miss Onazaki to send the man in. My

---

3. The truest likeness of her I've seen, Sato's face so pale that it seems to disappear. Only glancing very quickly at it, one might see no one at all.

Very soon, I imagined, she would move out of her mother's house for a second time, to live with a man, another man, who would be her child's father—a man whose features I often tried to imagine after that first morning.

My wife is still a very beautiful woman, Minister. Even more beautiful to me now, I think, as a result of our difficulties.

In contrast, my experiences have ground me into something not quite ugly but certainly less than noble or handsome, words many have used to describe my father and his brothers. I am not yet fifty, but when I step from my hot bath in the Uokai, Ltd. recreation facility and see myself in the mirror, the only part of my body that still appears remotely healthy is my hair. It is barely containable. All my life it has grown straight up from my head, in a great shock, so that all I can do to keep it from falling in every direction in an embarrassing and unprofessional way is to oil it well and brush the entire mass straight back, until it perches like a great rolling wave, poised to break against the faces of those around me. My body is rather unfit to support this phenomenon; it is not wrinkled or worn by any means, but quite thin. A poor, wrought-iron pedestal for such an immense sculpture.

4. He had, I learned later, labored up the nineteen flights of stairs to my office instead of waiting for one of the building's four elevators to return to the lobby. This is a breach of Uokai, Ltd.'s etiquette policy, as outlined in Appendix 6 of the *Uokai,*

office door had barely shut behind him before he began telling me his business.

"I am sorry," he said, wheezing. "I am sorry. I am very, very sorry to disturb you, Ito-san."

His tone alarmed me, and I finally looked up to discover who this heavy breather was, only to see the gentle if expansive double curve of his denimed buttocks, like the hills above Kyoto, raised to the ceiling before me, my visitor having bent double, bowing so deeply that his head nearly touched the floor. Though this grotesque display of supplication helped me to regain my composure somewhat, it was not enough for me to send him away, as I surely would and—in light of the consequences that have subsequently led to this report—should have done. But it was enough to make me realize I should never have let him in to begin with.

"Well?" I demanded.

He stood upright and I saw that he was Oshibori Saburo, a man in sad shape really, with a tendency toward excess and rather poorly schooled in social behavior. All the same, he is one of our sharpest buyers. I recognized him, in fact, from a photo in the most recent company newsletter, announcing him as employee of the month. He said he needed me to accompany him back to Tsukiji.

"A joke?" I asked, smiling. And truly, Minister, I did believe he was joking. I thought perhaps someone had mistaken 21 April for my birthday. I was, in fact, on the verge of laughing, in spite of the awkwardness of the moment, a moment of creeping anarchy, which at any other time I would have found wholly unacceptable.

But he was not joking. "No, Ito-san," he said. "There is a problem. Very serious. Your presence and personal opinion are required. I must demand that you come with me immediately."

Ltd. Personnel Manual, but as I have noted, I was sufficiently preoccupied with my own personal affairs and, eventually, with those of "The Tuna Affair," that I never thought to make an official report of the matter.

Demand? I can tell you, Minister, that I was quite perturbed by his audacity, employee of the month or no. Before I could rebuke him for it, however, I noticed that Saburo's hands were quivering. In and of itself, this is not an unusual physical state for someone of Saburo's rank in the presence of someone of mine (at Uokai, Ltd., in any case), and considering the exchange that had just passed between us, it would not have been unpleasant to me. But I also noticed that Saburo's quivering hands were wet, as were his face and his unkempt hair, so much so that he was dripping all over my carpet.[5] His jacket, however—besides those areas catching some of the significant moisture dripping from his head—was completely dry. An odd sight, to be sure.

It seemed reasonable to assume that Saburo's hands were still damp from evaluating tuna prior to that morning's auction. His head, however, was quite another matter.

I swiveled in my chair to look out the wide glass wall behind me. The sun had not yet risen over the hills of Chiba, and Tokyo Bay lay all dark below us, its edges chased by glittering highway lights and the fixed stars of East Bay factories, refineries, and power stations, an unbroken strand of light curving south to the point at Futtsu. Around the lighthouses, Kannonzaki and Suzaki, the fleets of freezer trawlers, rinsed clean, newly born and loosed from the docks, would guide themselves through the narrow passage of Uraga Strait and out into the cold, open space of the sea and the Catch. I watched them, the ghostly flotilla, a sort of zodiac of commerce, one ship distinguishable from the others over the dark distance only by the unique constellation of its running

---

5. The Minister will be unaware of the great personal significance of this carpet. I had it installed in my office (the largest of all of Uokai's department heads) within the week after I assumed my position as Head of Tuna. Sato had chosen the particular design: a somewhat random pattern of swirls and twisting white lines printed over an exquisite blue-green, the exact color of the Pacific Ocean as it appears far from shore. My wife often called me, in our first months here, "The Master of the Sea," as all day I lorded it over her ocean from behind the great cherrywood continent of my desk.

lights: the Dragon of Ryushu Oroshiuri; the Mole of Hozenkai, PLC; the Tuna of Uokai, Ltd.

A tattered canopy of clouds crept east across the sky. There was no rain yet, though it had been predicted.

I swung back around. Saburo seemed somewhat deflated now, listing to one side, his head lolling like a bored child's, as if he'd forgotten where he was, why he'd come in the first place. His hair continued to taunt me for several silent moments, a black and tangled storm troubling my ocean.

"Sweat," I deduced at last. Saburo snapped upright and began adjusting his coat. He swabbed his forehead with a stained and crumpled handkerchief.

"Senkai-san?" I asked then, as it seemed probable that the initiator of Saburo's "demand" was perhaps Uokai's chief executive officer.

"Kimura-san sent me," he said.

Kimura. This, as surely as if Saburo had answered my question about Senkai-san in the affirmative, was sufficient to preclude any further interrogation on my part.[6] I rose and motioned for him to lead me to the problem.

Miss Onazaki followed us as far as the elevators, asking when I would return, where she should say I was if anyone called, and would I be needing my overcoat. I allowed Saburo to answer for me. He revealed nothing to her about "The Tuna Affair."

By the time we reached the street, the dawn-lightening sky had darkened under the clouds, and a fine mist drifted down over us. Chuo Ward had already succumbed to the daily flood of traffic with its confusion of tides, currents, and crosscurrents—garbage trucks and buses,

---

6. I should note here, in case the Minister has not heard of him, that Kimura Maguroböchö is the finest tuna cutter in all of Tsukiji. Which is to say, in all of the world. Be assured that if Kimura has a problem requiring my assistance, it must be very grave indeed. Upon hearing of this situation, it was my duty, as an employee of Uokai, Ltd., to answer Kimura-san's summons. It is every employee's duty to do so, as the Minister will note should he examine page one of the *Uokai, Ltd. Personnel Manual*.

taxis, vans, legions of bobbing black umbrellas, salarymen and jump-suited market workers on mopeds and bicycles, helmeted and masked and sheathed in bright leather, vinyl, plastic, foul-smelling steam, sizzling neon and its distorted reflection on the oily, rain-slick pavement—all of which our wizened taxi driver navigated gracefully while fiddling with the radio. From out of a cloud of static another prediction of rain emerged, then a stock market report, news of a suicide, and then, like a little lost bird, a gentle flute melody. As the sky grew even darker and the mist turned to a light rain, other instruments, electric instruments, began to mimic the original tune, obscuring it until it became too complex for me to follow. An adolescent-voiced girl was singing about love, occasionally resorting to English words—*girlfriend, boyfriend, kiss, dance*—and I realized that I had left my office with the framed photograph of Sato still in my hand. I caught Saburo staring at her, the tip of his tongue twitching at the crusted corner of his mouth. He turned away when he saw that I'd seen him. He mumbled an instruction to the driver. I slid the portrait under my overcoat, face down.

Of course, upon review, it was easy to see how my wife could have maintained a clandestine affair. At Uokai, Ltd., as with every other interest at Tsukiji, an employee's day is the rest of the city's night. I arrive at my office at two o'clock each morning. I return home between half past eleven and twelve noon. Then I eat dinner, after which I spend approximately thirty minutes exercising, forty minutes bathing, and one hour reading. Occasionally I will also spend a few minutes in meditation or prayer. Then I sleep. Naturally, these activities are subject to preemption by more pressing matters, such as medical appointments, the renewal of licenses, and the filing of tax forms.

Within a month of our arrival in Tokyo I could sense Sato's displeasure with this schedule. She raised no verbal complaints at first, only trying to delay my early rising with kisses and intimate caresses, sometimes going so far as to whisper her wishes for a few rather exotic pleasures I had never previously known her to desire. Naturally, I did what I could to alleviate these longings, though not without an eye on the clock. I urged her to return to sleep, to suspend her passion until the afternoon when I could discharge my husbandly duties—joyful duties, Minister!—at a more leisurely pace. But how many times was I left disappointed, returning to find Sato unresponsive, even growing petulant when I kissed her ear or neck or fondled her in the most harmless and playful way? And when I attempted to make light of her change of attitude she only became more irritable. She accused me of badgering her, of treating her like a whore. When she responded in this way, I retreated to my study or to the bath. I had no desire to aggravate her further, and perhaps, I thought, she was only feeling homesickness or a slight imbalance of another, more routine physiological sort. As such turnabouts occurred with increasing frequency, however, I began to doubt the sincerity of her initial advances and chose to respond by spurning her flirtations altogether, whether I believed them to be sincere or not, hoping to curb her of any inauthenticity. Disagreement in the bedroom turned to argument at the dinner table, hurtful glances before the mirror, insults in the rock garden. It seemed that no part of our marriage was without conflict. Soon Sato was accusing me of being ruled by my work, of not loving her, of having an affair with Miss Onazaki.[7] And though I would attempt to produce evidence to refute these highly theatrical charges, I repeatedly found myself in a losing situation. My work schedule was the battleground, and for defending it I was guilty of hard-heartedness.

The simplest solution, it seemed, was for Sato to adjust her schedule to mine. But again and again, depending on the tone of our discussions, she would tell me either she wasn't able or didn't want to do this.

---

7. Whom she had met only once, but in whose manner she sensed an attraction to me with as much ease as if the poor woman had talked of nothing else. I myself was surprised at the swiftness of Miss Onazaki's attachment and somewhat embarrassed (for her) by her inability to conceal it.

Though Sato had been a highly paid and respected accounts manager in America, upon receiving notice of my promotion to Head of Tuna we had decided—after her initial suggestion, I should add—that when we moved to Tokyo she should take advantage of my generous salary and return to school. And this she did, following no particular course but rather pursuing a general study of Japanese culture, about which she still had much to learn. She enrolled in language, literature, and history courses at Waseda University. I hired a private tutor to teach her calligraphy.

But as my schedule continued to cause discord between us, I asked Sato to forgo her studies in favor of returning to work, despite Uokai, Ltd.'s rule that wives of men holding the rank of department head and above should not hold employment.[8] This was the final compromise I could offer. But my wife refused, insisting that she enjoyed what she referred to as her "idle life." She couldn't possibly return to work. She preferred, she said, the freedom to go shopping in the afternoons with the neighborhood ladies, to go to movies or read or watch television in the evening. All of these were part of her so-called cultural education, which, she always pointed out, I had previously encouraged.

Though it was not unusual during dinner (her lunch) for Sato to recite long tales about what this friend of hers did, what happened to that friend, who she had planned an outing with that evening, or, on occasion, who was coming to dine with us, I had never realized, until her refusal of my final offer, the extent of the social life she had constructed independent of the few hours we spent alone together at home—mostly, I think, because I rarely met any of her friends more than once. Not that I would have remembered them if I had.

My ignorance of this situation may seem like indifference. The Minister may, in fact, doubt the great affection for my wife that I have previously expressed. "What sort of fellow," the Minister may ask, "can love his wife so much as this man has said, and yet allow himself to be

---

8. *Uokai, Ltd. Personnel Manual*, XVII, viii.

so absorbed by his work as to not only force her into a double life, but also be unaware that he has done so?"

Minister, as regards the nature of my character, I am unable to answer. I can only say that my love for Sato was not any less because of my long hours away from her, and that, inversely, my long hours away were not a reflection of a lack, or diminution, of my love. On the contrary, had I not known, or at least expected, that she would be at home, or would soon be there, when I returned from work, I would surely never have achieved the success that I have. That is to say, during my relationship with Sato I have reached the highest pinnacles of my professional strivings.[9]

I value the sensual as much as any man, and the abundant pleasures of companionship, the radiant joy of forging a lasting spiritual union with a woman, but my manner has always been to allow my official duties to dictate the time allotted to personal pleasures. Can one still label me indifferent if he knows that in executing my daily duties I viewed the completion of every task as a demonstration of devotion to Sato, a gift given as the warrior once gave a poem, a noble death, the transient beauty of a moonlit vista? Perhaps my true fault lies in assuming that this attitude was properly understood.

Saburo and I entered the Tokyo Central Wholesale Market at approximately 7:45 on the morning of 21 April. Tsukiji was hurtling toward the final half of its day. Bicyclists and ta-rays careened through the crowd, the men and the machines all seeming to balance equally great numbers of cages, crates, and boxes. Cranes groaned on the docks, loading and unloading hauls of flash-frozen fish from every sea, lake, river, pond, bay, and ocean around the world—redfish and Atlantic cod,

---

9. As described in my last annual review: "[T]o acquire and distribute the freshest sushi-grade marine products to the greatest number of customers, without fear of contamination or imperfections, fulfilling our great social responsibility to provide the Nation with a stable and healthy diet, while maintaining the highest possible profit margin for Uokai, Ltd."

albacore, fugu, king and queen mackerel, flounder, swordfish, shark and salmon, herring, roughy, walleye pollock. Tuna.

Lights flashed and sirens wailed. Engines and hydraulic systems hummed, creaked, and whined through their business, their sounds so in harmony with the human pandemonium that it seemed every object, every person, every breeze blowing ripples through the market's bright banners was somehow driven by the operations of a vast and covert system of flywheels, pistons, and spinning shafts.

The grandeur of this spectacle made me forget Sato for the moment, as well as the bother of having to leave my office. Tsukiji swirled around me, spread itself open before me, a voluptuous garden, solicitous, overripe with fish, meat, and produce, with the scent of two thousand flowers, with humanity, buyers and sellers, the seemingly innumerable rows of stalls and tables and stands and workers stretching away into the distance, in every direction, a great organic machine, oblivious to the existence of a larger world circumscribing it, regulating its systems.

There is no air in Tsukiji, Minister, only water, and one must learn to breathe it to survive: salty bay fog and the fresh spray of hoses, mist rising from the defrosting fish, steam from a teakettle. My socks grew damp as the wet sheen of the cement found its way through the unprotected seams of my soles. A pair of spirited women sifted through bins of beans and mushrooms, while nearby a man shook his head and washed shrimp. And there were younger ones, laughing as they chopped the heads off salmon, joking about the previous night's Swallows-BayStars baseball game. There were buckets of clams and oysters, quivering sardines, tanks of lobsters. From every restaurant came the smell of tempura and yosenabe, oyakodon, and kabayaki.

Young boys and women hand-rolled sushi for floor managers reading the newspaper on their break. They were all new men, these managers, a generation or more younger than myself, and I knew I would never know them. There was a time when, at every step through Tsukiji, I would have encountered a friend or an acquaintance. That was only a short while ago. The comings and goings of people in my business, as well as yours, Minister, are infinitely more swift and unambiguous than the fluctuations of the Catch.

But as quickly as I was delighted by Tsukiji that morning, I became resentful of it. This beautiful garden I had been admiring as if from a distance, the distance of Uokai's nineteenth floor, through an autumn haze of nostalgia, was, in fact, as it always had been: a wilderness, un-managed, writhing and unrestrainable, lacking any sense of modera-tion—a severely infectious condition that was evident in the afflicted countenances all around me, a condition that was, perhaps, as much to blame for my loss of Sato as any fickleness in her character or any act of seduction. If it was true, as I believed, that I had been sharing my wife with another man, I could not have been doing so with any equity, and this seemed even more shameful than sharing itself.

It is at such moments of despair, Minister, that the most devastating strain of regret sets its teeth in me. There, caught in the market's whirl-pool heart, my palm recalled the weight of Sato's breast. My nose knew the scent of her skin. The taste of her body slid across my tongue. Be-neath my raincoat, held fast against my ribs by the pressure of my arm, the portrait was still hidden, the frame's sharp edges stabbing me, the cool glass and lacquer giving me a sudden chill through my shirt. For the first time since receiving the news of Sato's collapse, perhaps even since her departure, I felt fully awake, grotesquely aware of myself in the world, this parallel world that I had never known existed. I saw my-self reflected in the fishy eye of a convex mirror: alone, foreshortened, shivering in damp ignominy.

I needed to get away, out to the street, but when I turned to Saburo he had disappeared. Looking on every side, I found myself boxed in by stacks of wire cages full of frogs, all heaped upon each other's bloated, filthy bodies, unmoving, indifferent, unblinking, staring out in whichev-er direction they'd happened to be facing when they were packed for shipment. But for the slight movements of their breathing, I would not even have thought them alive. One particular set of eyes stared out at me. They knew me.

Did I cry out at this horror, Minister? I meant to. Indeed, I covered my ears to block out a prolonged and horrific keening that sent the frogs into a panic. I heard my name in their wild croaking, in the strange rasping they made as they struggled to escape their fate. Then they were gone, spirited away by a great golden forklift.

And again I heard my name. It was Kimura, standing there in front of me where the frogs had been, Saburo at his side, and though it took me a moment to acknowledge them, they seemed to take no notice of my agitation. The tuna cutter, grisly in his spattered, slimy apron, inclined his head in greeting and motioned for me to follow him to our tuna stall. I obeyed. Though he and Saburo exchanged a few short words along the way, neither attempted to brief me further about "The Tuna Affair."

Three or four men were at work cutting up a large bluefin when we arrived, and I stopped to observe them. The fish was short but bulky. The healthy red meat of its belly was well marbled and looked particularly valuable. It appeared to be a very good buy, and the sight of it, as well as the air of deference I'd sensed from the workers when I arrived, helped to restore my composure. Indeed, watching the crew dismantle the fish with well-rehearsed ease made me ponder the speed with which chaos may turn to order, dread to tranquility, flesh to food—and vice versa—these seeming oppositions separated only by a thin membrane of circumstance—unstable contiguous states we inhabit and abandon at the whim of some force or condition beyond our control, as readily as water turns to ice turns to vapor and back again. Is it possible, Minister, that truth, too, is such a substance: not developing, as we may believe, from blind ignorance toward clarity and understanding, but rather suffering its nature to be more constantly, and randomly, remade?

What was the problem, I asked Kimura finally. This fish looked excellent.

He pointed to the back corner of the stall where another, larger fish lay on a low wooden table, beneath a makeshift canvas awning. The working men looked up at us, their gaze following the direction of Kimura's silent gesture. They looked back at me, then set to hacking the spine out of the open fish before them. Though I did not know what to make of these glances, they seemed to me more indicative of the seriousness of the situation than anything I had seen or heard thus far that morning.

The second tuna was massive, looking to be well over five hundred kilos. It would bring a very fine profit if the meat was as good as that of the first. Except for a slight strangeness in its eyes, the fish appeared to have no visible defects. I asked Kimura again, more pointedly, what the problem was, and I let it be known that it irritated me to see such a valuable fish being allowed to sit and stink. Kimura motioned for Saburo and me to stand close together over the tuna to block the view from the adjoining stalls. Giving me one final glance in preparation, he kneeled and shoved his thick fingers into the tuna, wedging them into the cut he had already made in its belly to halve it. Then he lifted. Minister, I do not have the words to describe the mixture of shock, sickness, and amusement I felt at what I saw when Kimura opened that tuna. I say amusement because as my initial horror receded, I was certain (more certain than when Saburo had first appeared in my office that morning) that someone was playing a joke. This feeling did not last long.

Inside was the body of a woman, naked, gutted, perfectly halved, just like the fish, from crotch to crown. She was not a midget, nor a girl, but a miniature adult female, in her late thirties, forty at the most, fully formed and developed with long black hair, her body perfectly proportioned to fit inside the skin of the fish. The tuna itself had no inner organs, no skeleton. It was apparent that its skin served only as an outer covering for the small woman inside and that what flesh there was to the fish was only a kind of padding to fill out its shape, so that it, the tuna, gave no sign to either fish or fisherman that it carried a woman inside, that it was anything other than an average bluefin tuna.

She was beautiful, Minister. The entire construction was masterful, so much so that it seemed shockingly organic. Perhaps the most horrifying aspect of the thing (even now I am uncomfortable with the term *monster*) was the naturalness of the woman's expression of anxious surprise, the slight tension remaining in her muscles, traces of emotions or instincts that seemed both human and less than human, heightening the ambiguity of her origin, her species. I had never seen her before, of course, this small woman, yet her features begged me to recall a name or a similar face, perhaps that of someone I'd encountered once, briefly, in a crowd, or seen on television. My initial physical sickness evolved into a spiritual one. Curiously, this death felt to me like a crime.

"Are there any others like this?" I asked Kimura. There were not.

I asked Saburo how much he had paid for it. "Five hundred sixty-three thousand," he said.

I cannot authorize the disposal of so costly a fish without consulting Senkai-san.[10] I told Kimura and Saburo to wrap up the tuna and lock it in a freezer.

"Instruct the other men not to say a word to anyone," I told Kimura. "Tell them to say nothing, or . . . "

But I did not know how to finish. What was the extent of the danger? With what could I threaten them that would keep them from telling even their wives? I turned to watch the men working. None of them spoke or looked up, though I was certain they felt my eyes upon them. It seemed to me that they were all anxiously anticipating the moment, later that day, when, their work complete, they would pass beyond the borders of Tsukiji, and perhaps at a supper table, perhaps at a bar, at least one of them would reveal something of our secret catastrophe. Nothing could prevent this. I turned back to Kimura.

---

10. *Uokai, Ltd. Personnel Manual*, II, ii.

"Just tell them," I said. "Tell them to say nothing. Tell them that no one must know about this until I have corresponded with Senkai-san."

Kimura and Saburo nodded their assent and then began preparing the false tuna for the freezer.

As I returned alone to Uokai's offices, I began to wonder if my initial assessment of "The Tuna Affair" had been too limited. Stunned as I was by the unique and troubling spectacle, I had concluded almost instantly that Saburo had purchased a single, quite remarkable, but defective tuna. On reflection, however, this seemed rather too simplistic, indeed too hopeful. One rarely discovers a rotten plum in isolation. Assuming what I had seen inside that one fish was possible, was it not then possible, or even probable, that Saburo was not the only buyer at that morning's auction who had purchased a tuna concealing a human form? What if someone else, at Uminami 36, perhaps, or Onaka Tokyo, had discovered a similar defect in one of their tuna? Wouldn't it be best to contact those companies to suggest that we combine our efforts to solve the problem before news of the affair reached the press, before any damage was done to our sales, or to the reputations of our companies?

But then there was the problem of how to inquire about the other companies' purchases without revealing anything of our own situation, or, if we took a more passive approach, of a potentially interminable wait for one or another of our competitors to come forward with such an inquiry themselves. And if Uokai, Ltd. were to take the latter course, then once details of the affair emerged, as they surely would, how might such a delay, however short, affect consumers' confidence in our products, our century-old commitment to safety and excellence?

On the other hand, what if our delay was not short after all? What if no other company came forward? What if we were, in fact, alone? One imprudent query from me could destroy Uokai, Ltd.

The horror of this thought drove me back to my first question. What if we weren't alone? What if, that day, the entire catch was tainted and fish like ours had come to port not only in Japan but also in China, in America and Africa, Europe and Australia? And then this too seemed absurd. If the entire world had indeed been stricken with such a crisis, overnight, one might add, I would certainly have heard of it much earlier and from someone more official than Oshibori Saburo. Tsukiji would have shut down long before I arrived.

No, I decided, I had to treat "The Tuna Affair" as an isolated incident until I had discussed the matter with Senkai-san. That tuna—our tuna, my tuna—had to be the only one. It was my problem. My problem alone.

When I reached my office, I locked the door and immediately began composing a memo to Senkai-san.[11] It read:

---

11. I should make some note here of the special relationship between our executive and his staff. None of us has ever met directly with Senkai-san. In fact, we have never even seen him. Each of his ten personal secretaries assure me that he is a pleasant man, but only the senior secretary, a man of great age and generosity, has ever heard the sound of Senkai-san's voice, and even this was many years ago and merely a matter of a single cough. (Two of the lesser personal secretaries discount the old man's claim as false, though between them they disagree on whether the falsity is deliberate or the fruit of senile dementia.)

I have been told that, in meetings, Senkai-san sits behind an opaque screen beneath which he passes slips of paper detailing his desires. The ten personal secretaries, sitting cross-legged in a row before the screen, pass each of Senkai-san's communiqués down their ranks, recording the messages and the date and time at which they were received in color-coded notebooks.

When a message reaches the tenth personal secretary, that man goes into the hall and hands it to a runner (traditionally one of the personal secretaries' eldest son), who in turn delivers it to the secretary of the first of our five senior vice presidents. The first senior vice president reads the message and then returns it to his secretary, who forwards it to the secretary of the next senior vice president, and so on. When the message is returned by the fifth senior vice president to his secretary, it is submitted in the same manner, through their secretaries, to Uokai's five vice presidents, and then, finally, it is sent to the secretary of the proper department head, of which, as you know, I am one. The process is time-consuming, but our records are unfailingly accurate as a result. Senkai-san is adamant about maintaining the purity of his firm.

Wondrous spring girl,
plowing your waves in fishes' form,
avoid the market!

I gave this to Miss Onazaki in a sealed envelope, instructed her to send it immediately, and then returned home for the remainder of the day on the pretense of a severe headache. Quite frankly, I was afraid of the possibility that another crisis, of whatever size, might arise before noon.

All afternoon, as I lay awake listening to the monotonous cascades of rain rushing down the high slope of my roof and their long splattering fall to the pavement, I pondered my two problems, feeling very much like a Russian chess champion set upon, for the sake of his country's proud tradition, by two foreign-made and inhuman opponents at once, each programmed to pursue very different styles of play. But soon the lateness of the day, too, joined the contest, and I was driven to shelter behind closed eyes and dreams.

The bare white walls began to ripple, I recall, their surface becoming luminous, like the open ocean on a night of the full moon, beneath a sparkling coverlet of light, the little waves churned into motion by the fluttering fins and tails of tuna. Some of the fish flashed about at the far end of the room, amid reefs of bright blooming cherry trees painted on

---

I once admitted, at a dinner party in honor of Senkai-san's birthday (though no one knows for certain how old he is), that when I was at university I fancied myself a poet, writing haiku for any occasion, sometimes at the request of others. During the following week, one by one, Senkai-san's ten personal secretaries approached me to verify that I had made the statement (which they all quoted exactly) and to inform me that Senkai-san found this very interesting and admirable.

"He, too, is fond of writing haiku," they said, smiling, allowing their eyes to drift upwards, toward the twenty-first floor. Since that time, all of Senkai-san's memos to me have been in the form of haiku, and I have been instructed that it is preferred I respond in kind.

This digression will explain the somewhat odd nature of the memos regarding "The Tuna Affair" that passed between Senkai-san and myself, which for the sake of accuracy I have reproduced here.

the folding screen, while others, or rather the men and women inside them, whispered incessantly to me, trying to explain how they'd gotten where they were. One or two of them begged me to return their sister.

"Speak up!" I cried out, finally growing angry at the insolence of the fishes' muttering. And I awoke.

I thought again of Mrs. Kamakura's message and wondered if Sato had had her child yet. Her mother hadn't said whether it would be a boy or a girl. I was about to rise, thinking I should call Sato to see if everything was all right, but then I stopped myself.

"The child isn't mine," I whispered. "Why should I call?"

The walls were calm and silent.

I laid my head down again and hid my face in the crook of my arm, though there was little need to block out what light remained of that gray day, a day that had yet to start in San Francisco. But I wanted, or rather needed, to imagine the child's face in the darkness, Sato's child by another man. I tried for some time but could not visualize a satisfactory mix of features. Always they were predominantly Sato's, too much like the little girl I'd seen once, during a visit to Mrs. Kamakura's, in a black-and-white photograph, with a broad chubby face and a little round mouth pursed in confusion, lingering between a smile and tears, captured by her mother's camera on the threshold of the back door into the kitchen, the waiting stove behind in the shadows, and a teakettle exhaling steam, as though breathing for the still child, while rare piles of snow melted around the wooden porch. On the back of the photograph: "San Francisco, February 1967." Sato was nearly two.

No, I knew that to achieve an accurate image of her child I would have to mix in the features of a lover. This treacherous line of thinking, however, a whirlpool of impossible memory, drew me deeper into darkness and back in time, beyond the birth of the child, beyond Sato's departure, beyond the child's covert conception, past Sato and her lover, panting, tangled in the sweaty, semen-fouled sheets of autumn, and even further. I imagined Sato in the park, beneath an umbrella, Sato at a shrine, on a bridge, by the Sumida River, Sato walking, talking, laughing with another man. The meeting of eyes and the first words of betrayal. What could those words have been, Minister? Are they always the same? And how long before her words became polluted with a confession of disaffection? With confessions of a new affection, a vagabond love, without forgiveness, beyond forgiving?

And then I must have been dreaming again because I saw that woman, my wife, all spined, curled inside her purple sea urchin's armor, sitting in the corner where there had been a chair, her venomous tines reaching toward me, taunting and warning me in the gentle current. I heard her, soft and invisible in her shell. I heard her the way she had been when she and I made love, the sounds of encouragement that let me know I had found the particular spot requiring attention. I recalled her movements, the shuddering of her thighs that made her giggle because her body had passed beyond her control, and I recalled other touches and whispers, encounters hovering out of time, until I had an eager and painful erection. As I became aware of it pulsing I heard her cry out as if I'd entered her and her tines parted and her shell flew open and I saw them there at last: Sato, howling like the most whorish pearl diver of Toba, urging him on, her tongue flicking in and out of his gasping, gaping mouth, his tree-like penis plunging into her, his tanned, muscled arms and legs hugging and pumping, her arms, her legs embracing his slick and glistening body, the body, Minister, of the most magnificent bluefin tuna one can imagine, churning the submarine world of my dreams into restless darkness and tears with the joyous shuddering festival fan of his tail.

On the morning of 22 April, when I arrived at my office, Miss Onazaki handed me my newspaper and two messages, one from Senkai-san, the other from Kimura. Senkai-san's read:

> *Morning mist obscures*
> *the pure spring peak. I await*
> *dreams of clarity.*

And Kimura's only this:

Come quickly.

I determined that it would be best if I saw Kimura first, in the event that whatever he had to tell me might help in a revised report to Senkai-san.

When I reached the tuna stall, I found our men sitting on folding chairs out front, smoking. They were not talking amongst themselves and did not speak to me or even look up as I approached. I was tempted to reprimand them for not working, as I would have under normal circumstances, but they looked rather more nervous than indolent, and, in any case, I did not want to give them any reason to revenge themselves upon me or on Uokai, Ltd. So I inclined my head to them and asked the nearest man where I might find Kimura. The man did not stand up. He laughed aloud, drawing the attention of workers from neighboring stalls, and then jerked his thumb over his shoulder. I couldn't imagine what this kind of behavior meant.

Kimura and Saburo were waiting at the back of the stall where they had shown me the tainted fish the previous day. Before them, on newspapers on the ground, lay three bluefin tuna, as large and larger than that of the day before. When I stepped up to them and asked why they had summoned me, the two men made no response. They looked at each other in silent agreement and then bent down to open up the fish at our feet.

Again their revelation filled me with a strange amalgam of emotions. Inside each fish lay a body, two men and a woman, perfectly proportioned, perfectly halved. This time, to my own surprise and, I'm sure, to the surprise of Kimura and Saburo, I laughed as I knelt down to inspect the bodies more closely. Shock, perhaps, was the cause, or an involuntary physical response to ward off sickness to the stomach. But the dry, sharp bark of it resonated, too, with that grudging, inarticulate response extended to an unpleasant relative who has surprised one with uncommonly polite greetings in a public place.

The first body was a man's. He looked to be about forty and was somewhat gaunt, with short hair. He reminded me of a village fisherman with his dark, deeply creased skin, what one might expect from extended exposure to the sun and salt air. A long pink scar was visible beneath his right kneecap. It curved round the outside of his leg, almost to the back.

The second man was an old grandfather, with white hair and a short, unkempt beard. He was quite handsome and more muscular than one might expect for someone his age, which I approximated at eighty. His skin was speckled here and there with dark spots of pigment, and his eyes showed the misty opacity of advanced cataracts.

The most curious of the three, however, was the woman. She was blond and perhaps in her early or middle thirties. Of the four bodies I had seen so far, hers was the only one that didn't look Japanese. She had plain features, a slight, unremarkable figure, and skin pale to the point that I could easily see the wide blue veins beneath the surface. Her seeming frailty, independent of the sizable tuna in which she lay, gave me a desire to touch her, and I heard Saburo gasp as I did. She was still cold, of course, still defrosting from being flash-frozen, but in all other respects her body seemed normal, even human. Had I been blindfolded, I might have believed myself to be touching the frostbitten hand of a very young girl.

"Where did this fish come from?" I asked Saburo.

"Boston, Ito-san," he said. "All three. Yesterday's also."

Glancing over them once more before forcing myself to look away, I felt as before, that I knew those faces, those bodies, something of them, individual features perhaps, and even more dreadfully, that they had at some time and with equal ambiguity known me.

"Wrap them up and put them in the freezer," I told Kimura. "And either find some way to get those men to work or send them home."

Four rotten plums. I returned to my office, all the while reconsidering my previous thoughts on whether or not to contact our competitors.

But I remained resolute in my decision to do nothing before receiving a definite statement from Senkai-san. As far as I could be certain, no one outside myself, Senkai-san, and the small group of men at our stall at Tsukiji knew about our problem. If, in fact, no one else knew, no one else had to know. I wrote Senkai-san another memo and gave it to Miss Onazaki, again in a sealed envelope. It read:

> *She wears the tuna*
> *coat still as Commerce plans her*
> *shipment—spring morning.*

For the rest of that day, I went about my normal business, perusing the reports of our distributors, foreign and domestic, and those of our dockside buyers overseas. To any outside observer, nothing would have appeared to be out of the ordinary. But, really, I was just waiting. I was waiting to hear from Senkai-san, waiting for another message from Kimura, waiting for Sato or her mother to call, waiting for a call from the press. Perhaps, Minister, though I would never have admitted it at the time, I was waiting for you.

At around five-thirty that morning I took my mandatory break to read the newspaper, and my waiting came to an end. On the front page was a lengthy article on a recent study of global fish populations, conducted by the Food and Agriculture Organization (FAO), an investigation prompted by the alleged leveling-off of annual numbers in the worldwide catch, as well as a number of fishery closures in the United States and Canada.

The findings of this study implied that stasis in the global catch was due to a general and significant decrease in the populations of some of the most sought-after fish. Shrimp, prawns, redfish, herring, salmon: all were reported to be in danger of extinction.

Of course, before this I was well aware of the decreases in the Catch and the accusations made by the West against our country in relation to this phenomenon. Normally, however, my concern was aroused solely to the extent that such a report might affect my section, which is to say, prior to reading about this FAO study it had never occurred to me that the overall population of the oceans might be declining. The overall population was none of my concern. On the contrary, I assumed, as I'm sure you and the majority of our countrymen did, that of all Japanese industries, fishing was the most stable, that Japan would never suffer for fish.

But perhaps I have not been clear enough. I said that after reading this article my waiting had come to an end. Rather, I had only begun to believe so.

After a moment of considering the implications of such studies concerning the industry as a whole, I began to wonder if the problem of depletion—assuming the studies represented an accurate and viable explanation for the alleged general stasis—was somehow linked with my local problem: the bizarre nature of four of our bluefin tuna.

I wrote the following memo to Senkai-san:

> *April moonlight wanes*
> *over silent waves. Darkness*
> *asks: Where are the fish?*

Standing in the doorway of my office, however, my arm already half raised to hand the new poem in its envelope to Miss Onazaki, I reconsidered sending it and decided instead to wait for Senkai-san's response to my last memo before forwarding my hypothesis. I was speculating, after all. I had no reason other than their coincidence to believe that the two phenomena were related, "The Tuna Affair" and the decrease in oceanic populations—reported, but not by any means proven—and I thought again of the possible damage that mounting a premature investigation—whether internal or industry-wide—might do to Uokai, Ltd.'s reputation. Better to wait for a time, I told myself, to see if any more of the strange fish turned up in our stall or someone else's, or if the FAO's findings were confirmed, perhaps months or years from now, either as fact or merely as the prelude to another American-led economic attack. Perhaps, after all, as has always been the case, the Catch would recover, and in the meantime our "affair" would resolve itself.

At any rate, I needed to ponder the question further, to think ahead and determine, in case the time came for me to make a recommendation for action, what connection there might be between the FAO's report and the bodies in our fish. This was my responsibility to Senkai-san and to Uokai, Ltd.[12]

But there sat Miss Onazaki, staring up at me, blinking, as though she expected something more than just the secret communiqué I was almost holding out to her. I noticed she had undone an extra button on her blouse.

"Ito-san?" she asked.

I was caught for a brief but awkward moment between thoughts, between possibilities. I could not think of anything proper to say, yet something needed to be said.

"Have you any children, Miss Onazaki?" I asked. She looked away, toward the door leading out to the hallway, then down at her knees. She began to quiver a little just as Saburo had, but without sweating.

"I'm not married, Ito-san," she said.

"Yes, I know that." I also glanced at the door, but it was too late. "Have you any children?" I asked again.

"No," she said. "No, I haven't any children."

What could I do then, Minister? I backed into my office and shut the door. Too hard, I think. After a few moments I heard the door of the women's toilet open and then close.

I slipped the unsent memo into the bottom right-hand drawer of my desk and laid the portrait of Sato on top of it. The previous moment's encounter had unnerved me. I could not stand to return, now, to my stance of waiting for movement on any front, allowing absurd questions to emerge from my mouth unchecked. If I was to sit still regarding

---

12. *Uokai, Ltd. Personnel Manual, XXX,* iv.

"The Tuna Affair," I was determined to take positive action in my dealings with my wife.

I drew a blank sheet of paper from the drawer and began to write Sato a letter.

Dearest—

I don't know if you intended for me to learn about your child, but, as you may or may not realize, your mother called my office to inform me that you had gone into labor at the local market. I hope the delivery turned out well.

Why didn't you tell me you were going home? Perhaps you didn't know yourself when you left, but surely you could have contacted me after you'd arrived. I would not have tried to stop you. Not at all. Rather, it would have been enough for me to know you were happy, wherever, and with whomever, you needed to go.

I won't lie to you, however, and let you assume from these pleasantries that I am well. I have had a very hard time without you, though the last two months have been better, only because I determined that I must do my best to forget everything about you. I have destroyed all my pictures of you, as well as those clothes and sundry items you left behind. I have moved to a much bigger house, out in the country, where you always wanted to live, so I am not at work nearly as much as I used to be.

I have also embarked on several very satisfying sexual affairs simultaneously, so, as you can imagine, I haven't much time for work in any case.

But then I received the news from your mother. Again I ask, why didn't you tell me? There was no need to try to hide your affair. In fact, I was aware of it the entire time. I would have granted you a divorce and even financed your move had you asked me openly. I would have been rather glad to get free of you, for you never provided me with that happiness for which I once believed you had the potential.

But now, I'm afraid, your insistence on lying and your pitiful attempts at deception, however poorly executed (I believe I gave you every opportunity to tell me the truth), have eclipsed any hope you might have of financial assistance from me for yourself or your baby. You have shamed me, and so much the more by sneaking back to America to have your lover's child.

In spite of my prior knowledge of your infidelity, however, I was quite angry to learn of your pregnancy, I'll give you that. Perhaps it is indicative of the overwhelming disappointment I felt at your untruth that I neglected to consider the likely, indeed the biologically certain, result. I did not think you would stay with your other man for so long.

You are right, you know (you always were), to think me self-centered. This trait, I'm sure, was at the bottom of my belief in the transient nature of your love affair. I believed that, though you may have thought you were seeking happiness, you were in fact, if perhaps unconsciously, trying to hurt me, and that you would tire of this trite exercise once you realized it was having no effect.

But perhaps you truly were seeking happiness. You have shown me my folly. Thank you. (But then, I would have to assume your man is still with you. Is he?)

It's a pity that when I received your news I had nothing of yours left to destroy but a chipped porcelain teapot, forgotten by us both on a high cupboard shelf. Such a small vessel for so great a wrath was simply not acceptable. I was forced to vent the abundant excess on others, orally reprimanding my underlings, even striking some of them, and tormenting Miss Onazaki by seducing her and then publicly ridiculing her love for me. I've also run down several small animals, pets mostly, near my new country home. Generous gifts have made my neighbors understanding.

I laid down my pen. Was this the way to go about writing a letter to my wife? Did I really believe, to the extent that I was giving the idea credence, that she'd had an affair? That she still was? Or was this a continuation of my attempts to cover the shame of having lost her? A shame redoubled now at the thought of losing a child as well, losing the possibility of our having one of our own, or even raising the one she'd had, whoever its father was, a child nonetheless, an innocent in the affair?

And what right had I to speak so of Miss Onazaki, another innocent, who I have already told you was a devoted worker and nothing less, despite the folly of her love for me? Ah, Minister, the transitory nature of certainty, the imprecision of people, ideas, things—how they can impassion us for one season, frustrate, even destroy us the next. I left the letter unfinished and went to check on Miss Onazaki.

She had returned to her desk and was transcribing a message from one of our vice presidents. I stood in the doorway to my office waiting for her to turn around, as she always did when she heard my door open. A minute passed, then two. I continued to wait. I began to fear that I had finally lost the love of Miss Onazaki now too, a love that I had come to depend on as much as Sato's, if not for its substance at least for its constancy. I grew more and more anxious as the ticking of the wall clock filled the room with empty seconds. But I was determined not to speak. That would have been asking too much.

After several minutes, I turned to go back into my office. Not until my door had swung closed did I hear Miss Onazaki say, very meekly, "What is it you wish, Ito-san?"

"Come in," I called out, hurrying to be seated behind my desk. The door opened. She had rebuttoned her blouse. Her eyes still glittered with one or two tears.

I slowly stood and motioned for her to take her customary seat in one of the chairs across from mine. As she did this, I turned to my window and inspected the bay. The rising sun over Bōsō-hantō transmuted the leaden water into shimmering brightness with the first touch of its light. I took several deep breaths. Restored now to her proper orbit, Miss Onazaki too, I felt, bestowed some peace and clarity upon the dark waters of the past two days. I asked if she thought it would rain over the coming weekend.

When she made no response, I turned and found her staring at me, her face lacking any definite expression. This surprised me. I had felt certain, as I spoke, that my words would have an immediate and obviously ameliorating effect upon Miss Onazaki. In fact, I enjoyed the thought of keeping my back to her for a few additional moments, postponing the pleasure that I would receive on seeing her face, joyous at the implications of the familiarity of my tone. But this was arrogance. Even now, as I recall the cold inscrutability of her expression while she calculated the risks and probabilities involved in her response, I am ashamed that, in my letter to Sato, for the sake of histrionics, I presumed to underestimate Miss Onazaki's character. Obviously there was still work to be done to restore true harmony to our relations.

"You are a very dependable worker, Miss Onazaki," I told her, returning to my seat. "I am sorry not to have recommended you for commendation or promotion earlier. It is difficult to part with an associate I depend upon as much as I depend upon you, but I will talk to the necessary people immediately." Of course, I had no intention of "parting" with Miss Onazaki. I only meant to placate her, knowing that even with a promotion I could somehow retain her presence in my office.

She nodded her head once, but strangely she did not leave. Again a vexing awkwardness plagued me, and I understood that still something more was required, perhaps a small gift or an act of kindness. I continued to speak as if I had intended to inquire all along:

"Have you a car, Miss Onazaki?"

"No, Ito-san," she said. "I take the train to work."

We sat in silence.

"Well, perhaps today you would like to take a taxi home," I suggested. "Please call one for yourself and I will give you the fare."

Again there was silence. Looking into Miss Onazaki's black, slow-moving eyes, I was reminded of the daily dockside deals in which I had engaged as a young employee, and a vestigial reflex was reawakened in me, a reflex seasoned and conditioned during those countless bargaining sessions over fresh catches with men all over the world—the sportsmen, the amateurs, the professionals, the sophisticated, the near starved. But that was many years ago, Minister. I recognized the game I was in, yes, but far too late. I had already been hoisted up on the scale, and the cash-only transaction was all but complete.

"Or," I surrendered, "perhaps we could ride together."

We had reached the final gambit, Miss Onazaki and I. She knew as well as I that I would not, could no longer, risk her coldness. And so I had nothing left to offer her but myself. The sun continued to rise behind me. I could feel it on the tips of my ears. I could see its light warming in Miss Onazaki's eyes.

"Yes," I said. "We will ride together to your home, and after you have changed into more casual attire, perhaps we could have dinner in celebration of your imminent promotion. 'If, of course, you think that is all proper and agreeable.'"[13]

"Yes, Ito-san," Miss Onazaki said. She sat for another moment, nodded her thanks again, then rose and left in silence, drifting across my green sea like a delicate origami flower sailing the golden course of the sun's rising.

By noon that day, I had still heard nothing from Senkai-san regarding "The Tuna Affair." For the first time since we'd begun working together, Miss Onazaki and I rode the same elevator to the lobby. Without any prior discussion about the matter, we stood apart from each other, allowing ourselves to be pressed into opposite corners by the usual chattering mass who could not have noticed the uniqueness of the situation. For my part, however, I felt awash in the moment's singularity. But I would not shrink from its immensity. How could I, Minister, after the stunning example of will displayed by my secretary? There was no denying her brilliance—the silence, Minister, her sublime use of silence!— but rather than feeling humiliated by her victorious maneuvers, I was inspired by Miss Onazaki. Thus far regarding "The Tuna Affair" I had acted exactly as I should, exactly as was expected of me by Senkai-san,

---

13. My closing remark phrased as per the recommendations of the *Uokai, Ltd. Personnel Manual*, Executive Addendum, Section C: "Propositional Etiquette."

by Uokai, Ltd., and by our customers. Doing so had brought me to an impasse, left me helplessly bound by fear and regulations. Miss Onazaki had acted swiftly, unexpectedly, even recklessly in her exploitation of my weakness, and in only minutes she had forged for herself a sort of Manchukuo of the heart. Within the cold confines of my defeat, admiration and a new determination unfolded like the late and lasting double-bloom of the Kwanzan cherry. I decided that on the morning of the following day I would produce and act upon a creative and decisive policy regarding "The Tuna Affair." In the meantime, I carried in my briefcase the unfinished letter to Sato, which I would mail later that afternoon. Once matters with Miss Onazaki had been settled, however they were to be settled, I would conclude the letter as I had intended, with a permanent farewell, while also expressing due regrets to Sato and the child, using a more respectful, less strident tone than the one I had been building toward in my earlier, less rational state.

During a brief pause at the eleventh floor as more workers squeezed onto the elevator, I allowed myself a quick glance at Miss Onazaki. She was nodding her head in greeting to a female acquaintance who was waiting in line to enter and did not see me. Miss Onazaki's demeanor was entirely professional, but she also emanated a relaxed joy that put me at ease and, moonlike, seemed to draw the nearly immovable throng toward her, a human neap tide, unfocused, harmless, and broadly benevolent. Among the many things the insensate crowd in that elevator would probably never realize, I thought with some sadness, was the quiet instructional value of workers like Miss Onazaki.

In my corner, as always, my elevated status buffered me from them all, but I could see that, drawn as they were to Miss Onazaki, I too exerted some attractive force upon them, that they struggled against my buffer, that the mysterious aura of "The Tuna Affair," the scent, as it were, of imminent positive action—as intoxicating as the scent of the finest tuna to the gourmet—agitated the workers around me. Their heads pivoted a bit restlessly and their eyes rolled, their lips struggled with unutterable pleas and invitations, their glances grew more nervous, excited, anxious as they tried to follow or ignore one another's twitching fingers and fluttering hands, while staying aware of me, yearning for me to be aware of each of them. They seemed, Minister, like a school of mackerel, sparkling, darting, flashing this way and that, giddy with the fatal intensity of half-finished lives suddenly darkened by the shadow of a swiftly descending, predatory end. Only then did I begin to understand my private knowledge of "The Tuna Affair" as an advantage, an enhancement if you will, rather than the burden I had supposed it to be. This was a realization I might never have had had I not engaged in that fateful encounter with Miss Onazaki. I did not attempt to conceal my erection.

During the taxi ride to her apartment, Miss Onazaki responded pleasantly to my questions about her family and her life, such as it was, outside the offices of Uokai, Ltd. I found myself smiling, even laughing at her witty observations about certain unpleasant coworkers I had never met. We avoided calling each other by name, perhaps aware that, though it might have been proper in such an intimate atmosphere, addressing one another as Hideo and Sadohara was not possible without evoking a certain amount of embarrassment, enough to disrupt our good spirits, even if only for a moment. Nevertheless, I recall thinking that we were making overtures to love, and this, in turn, reminded me of the claim about seducing Miss Onazaki that I had made in my unfinished letter to Sato. The lie troubled me, though I felt certain Miss Onazaki would welcome a seduction, even expect it, and I myself might have been the better for such a liaison, however brief. Still, I believed then as I do now that seduction is indeed a low art. I wonder if my belief that Sato had been, or was capable of being, receptive, not simply susceptible, to seduction, perhaps had even mastered its intricacies herself, was the source of my disappointment with her. For, at its root, the vitriol I heaped upon her in my most private thoughts represented my great disappointment in a person I had once held in the highest regard.

But love, Minister? Overtures to love? These small joys I had been sharing with Miss Onazaki revealed their transitory nature as we sat in traffic outside the Hanami Shopping Mall.

The sublime video of blooming cherry trees that scrolled across the video canopy above us, and the perpetual waves of synthetic blossoms washing over the street, overwhelmed our happy conversation and made us laugh with wonder. Miss Onazaki, resting her head on the seat, looked out of the taxi's rear window, up into the shower of petals, exposing the long, pale, smooth, inviting curve of her neck, and I began to lean forward, thinking, albeit with some trepidation, that, within the romantic paradigm I had noted earlier in our journey, this was an appropriate moment to kiss her there.

Then I saw a boy.

He had wandered out into the stopped traffic and was standing beside the cab, watching us. I began to draw back and Miss Onazaki turned to look at me, her eyes narrow, animal, full of passion, showing her recognition of my initial intent, then, tearfully human again, questioning my refusal, and finally, as she followed my gaze over her shoulder, widening with renewed wonder at the revelation of this boy, this interloper. He moved closer and stood on his toes, pressing his filthy nose to the glass.

"Poor child," Miss Onazaki said. She waved, but he did not react. "He's lost his mother."

"Or his father," I said. "Or both."

The boy was perhaps three, no more than four, with a fat face and wet eyes that roamed over us and the whole of the taxi's interior. It did not appear that he was asking to be let in. Indeed, he didn't seem to be asking anything. He only gaped. The urge to investigate would come later, if at all. My tenuously high spirits, as well as their physical manifestation, withered beneath his cold, dumb scrutiny.

"Perhaps he hasn't any parents at all," I continued. I did not deliver this analysis with the tone of philosophical reverie one might expect from such a ridiculous statement. Rather, I spoke with the voice of Commerce, too rapidly, too harshly, with too much certainty. Miss Onazaki looked at me with an expression of concern for a troubled friend, but then, seeing the seriousness of my stare, looked away, perhaps sensing in me a secret imbalance, the hint of a deep, pathological belief in the notion that some children simply appear, emerging from a cloud of false cherry blossoms to wander the streets of Tokyo acting a nuisance.

"There's a sad thought," she said as the cars ahead of us began to move and those behind sounded their puny horns. A man and a woman trotted through the storm of petals before we pulled away. The man grabbed the child, lifted him up, and then we left them—father, mother, son.[14] The boy's muscular wails trailed us for more than half a block.

"What a child that would be," Miss Onazaki said in a voice I was perhaps not meant to hear.

Confronted again by impertinent muttering, I was finally unable to control myself. "What was that?" I demanded. Adding more gently, "Hideo." And I reached for her, Minister, arching my trembling fingers so that I almost touched her small fist, tight and cool on her thigh. I could sense its need for warmth, that small object of destiny, struggling to open, to accept the unlikely promise of my touch. We were only observers, Miss Onazaki and I, watching our hands attempt this slow, pathetic Kabuki, until, too uncertain, we allowed our eyes to do what our hands could not.

Youth, Minister, that certain shine of youth, its glistening eyes and supple buttocks, its revealed knees and dubious posture, the sheen of its hair and the aqueous sensuality of its defiant, insubordinate gait—youth is a toxic garden of disconsolation and unearthly beauty. Miss

---

14. At least, that was how I thought of them. And neither Miss Onazaki nor, so far as I could tell, anyone in the cars around ours seemed to think otherwise, as no one stopped to interrogate them. It seemed natural, despite the recent rise in child abductions in Tokyo, to think of them as a family. Perhaps I'd misjudged the boy's intentions altogether. I suppose one can only wonder.

Onazaki, spangled with afternoon reflections, seemed to have no concern for anything but my good health. For me. She seemed more like a sad and beautiful young wife than a secretary. Such a fantasy! No one's bride. How changed she would be, I thought, on the day when all proper ceremonies had been performed and she was finally tethered to the groom for whom she was intended.

I turned my head, just slightly, and that ended the matter.

"Nothing," Miss Onazaki whispered, her little fist opening too late. "I said . . . I . . . I meant nothing." Was there apology in those breathy syllables? Regret? Acceptance? The sound was too slight for me to be certain. She raised her thin, cold hand, touched her ear, and twisted a small lock of hair, smoothing it slowly against her neck as she turned again to the window. "Ito-san," she said. All possibility of an affair between Miss Onazaki and me vanished at that moment. We knew our responsibilities. This illustrates the training one receives at Uokai, Ltd. I will tell you, Minister, that I am very proud to have served such an outstanding company. I feel nothing but shame, shame of the highest order at the difficulties my actions have brought upon it.

Miss Onazaki lives at the edge of Aifuku, a clean and secure neighborhood, I suppose, though somewhat aimless. There is very little real vegetation and all the buildings look the same—tall cliffs of beige concrete, narrow windows marking their faces at regular intervals, edifices like punch cards. The only bright colors are those pulsing across the massive video billboards advertising hygiene products, fruit juices, and popular novels, and those streaking the radiant pompadours of the skateboarders who pummel the neighborhood's small public meeting place beneath their wheels, often, quite gratifyingly, receiving equally harsh punishment as they tumble across their makeshift playground.

Most of the neighborhood's residents look alike, too. In fact, we passed a group of young women approximately the same age as Miss Onazaki, all of them dressed exactly like her: black, thick-soled loafers; tall white socks; pleated, blue knee-length skirts; white silk blouses; blue blazers bearing the crest of an imaginary girls' academy. Had I not spent so many years working with Miss Onazaki, I am sure I would not have been able to pick her out of this pony- and pigtailed crowd. The few young men I saw on the street looked as much like each other as the women, and some even like the women as well. Miss Onazaki waved to the girls as we passed. They waved back in unison.

"They are secretaries at Onaka Tokyo," she said. "We ride the train together every morning." I did not look back at them, knowing that every girl would now have a hand raised to her mouth and would be whispering to the girl next to her about Miss Onazaki in a taxi with an older gentleman. *Isn't he Ito, Uokai's Head of Tuna?*

Miss Onazaki asked the driver to leave her at the corner, where she could be overtaken by her friends, and we parted silently, without so much as a nod. I told the driver to go on quickly. I had no reason to expect, and had given no thought to, a more intimate farewell, but this, though it relieved us both of a certain amount of awkwardness, seemed rather insufficient.

Back home, at my door, I found a small overnight envelope mailed from San Francisco. It contained a letter and a photograph, one edge of which I'd torn off in my haste to open the package. The picture was of a baby wrapped in a blue blanket, cradled in a woman's arms. The woman was Sato. The baby's face was slightly blurred. It looked up at me with black, unfocused eyes, and still I could not tell if the child was mine.

The enclosed letter was handwritten in English on a single sheet of paper.

> *Sadohara—*
>
> *I am sorry for taking so long to write to you, sorry that news of my pregnancy had to reach you in the way it did. Have you looked carefully at the picture? Our son is a healthy, pleasant child. I have named him Kashi, but write us soon and tell me if that doesn't suit you. I'm sorry he wouldn't smile for you. If he had, you would see how much of yourself is*

in him. His face, when he laughs, is so like yours that I am caught between laughing myself and a deep sadness for what has passed between us. I say sadness, not regret. I was too unhappy, Sadohara. I had to leave. But you must believe that, at the time, I didn't know I was pregnant—and once I'd discovered the truth, it seemed too late to return. You must believe this. No matter how unpleasant our life had become, I never would have left had I known about the child.

Expect to see us soon. No definite date or duration for our visit. When things are well, we will see you.

Love—
Sato

I felt the prickling birth of tears and immediately I was weeping. As one might assume, Minister, I was so surprised by the letter, by the photograph, so moved, that I was ready to believe every word. Though I had only the previous morning been wishing for some change of heart like this in Sato, I could not, knowing the strength of her determination in all things, could never have believed she would consider returning to me. And yet, here it appeared that she might. A child, unexpected, had been the difference.

Remembering my earlier resolve to send her the cruel letter I still carried in my briefcase, I pulled it out now and was about to throw it in the trash in favor of something more appropriate to my incipient joy, but, instead, I added a brief codicil on the back:

In the end, my dear, my only wish is that you should return to me, even if only for a little while. I would like the opportunity to see the child. We three could go on holiday to the western sea.

Or, if this would be too difficult, perhaps I could come to you. I have, as you always believed and I too often denied, thought frequently of San Francisco and wondered if I would ever return. I had given up hope of doing so, but perhaps now I could.

There should be no need to conceal from Sato my earlier, vituperative state of mind. Better, I thought, that she should decipher my change in attitude for herself.

Putting my letter aside for the next morning's post, I examined again the photograph Sato had sent. This was my son, she'd said. He had a significant amount of black hair, as was the case with several members of my family at birth, myself included, but besides this the child looked to me like any other newborn, and this suddenly made me skeptical.

Babies just out of the womb are of a kind, a homogenous class of being all their own, the specific physical traits of father and mother only emerging from that chaos of instincts, urges, and uncontrollable functions over time. Yes, I could tell myself today that this was my son, convince myself of it in the hopes that such faith would eventually bring back my wife and simultaneously give me a family. But perhaps one evening my reason would catch me, or rather Sato, in a lie. Perhaps I would look at him, *my boy*, puzzling over a school assignment, some equally odious and impenetrable equation, and think, "I have grown accustomed to your having more of your mother in you than me. But your chin, that curl in your hair, whose are they? Not mine, certainly. Who are you, boy? Whose?"

My tears returned, slowly, thick, warm, forced out by the vicious rage welling up behind them. "Bitch!" I screamed, tearing Sato's letter and my own into a hundred pieces. She could say whatever she wanted about the baby, knowing that I would want to believe her, knowing that, later, when the facts of the boy's body might prove her a liar, my attachment to him would be too strong to break. She could say she hadn't known she was pregnant when she left. She could absolve herself of all wrongdoing, knowing that I would want her back regardless. She could say anything.

I tore the letters into even smaller pieces.

But Sato had always known exactly what she was doing, what she wanted, what she needed. With some relatively minor exceptions, I think I could say we had this in common. How was it, then, that in this instance she was negligent? She hadn't known she was pregnant? Impossible, Minister! Impossible! This impossibility, finally, was the most significant barrier to my accepting Sato's explanations.

I watched the tiny pieces of our letters fluttering in the air, dancing across the carpet. Before the last of them had settled, I was telephoning Kimura.

Positive action, Minister. Positive action. To exert one's will no matter the consequence, to inhabit a crisis or negotiation, to abide in the small, golden temples of my industry as I have inhabited my office, when necessary, for days, even weeks, with little sleep, as those bodies, once living, inhabited our strange tuna, my tuna, breathing through their gills, witnessing the deep, the other world, through sea-formed lenses, every orifice, organ, and function modified for existence in that vast, violent darkness: this was the only sensible course. One must, after all, exert control where one can, and, as Head of Tuna, my realm was not the boudoir but the market.

I told Kimura to start cutting up the questionable tunas the next morning. I told him to inform Saburo that he should seek out distributors as always.

"What about the other business?" Kimura asked me, his tone betraying no lack of courage. It was a question asked as plainly as if he had asked me the time. I knew, as I had always known, that Kimura would not balk at my orders.

"Sell it all," I told him.

On the morning of 23 April, I arrived at my office promptly at two o'clock. Miss Onazaki was busy filing an immense stack of forms and memos that had accumulated overnight, but she paused just long enough to wish me an unsuggestive good morning while handing me my late-edition *Asahi* and a sealed communiqué from Senkai-san.

Still uncomfortable about our shabby leave-taking the previous evening, I lingered near her desk, pretending to peruse the headlines, wondering how, with a word, I might return us to that moment so that we could complete it properly. But Miss Onazaki had already resumed her filing. I was once again Head of Tuna. Miss Onazaki was my secretary. There was nothing to add. I hurried into my office and shut the door.

Senkai-san's communiqué read as follows:

> *Iris and bee know*
> *the cherry's snow from winter's.*
> *In spring, I care not.*

On the reverse side of the parchment was another note, in the senior secretary's handwriting. It read: "Senkai-san has instructed me to inform you to cheer up."

It was apparent to me then that Senkai-san still knew nothing of "The Tuna Affair" and that, if anything, my second attempt to explain the problem had been even more obscure than the first. Perhaps he felt my correspondence was merely personal, having to do with my wife. Whatever his intentions, I did not respond to his message, and I determined not to make any more mention of "The Tuna Affair" to him until I had constructed a solid base for discussion of the matter.

For nearly two weeks afterward, the status of "The Tuna Affair" remained stable and our operations at Tsukiji continued without difficulty.[15] But all the confidence I gained from this stability disintegrated on the morning of 5 May as I sat pondering the April market report,

---

15. So far as I knew. I had no contact with any of our employees there but Kimura, and my telephone conversations with him consisted only of daily confirmations that:

    a) the bodies were a continued and increasingly frequent presence in our tuna,

    b) all the men employed at our stall at the beginning of "The Tuna Affair" were still accounted for,

    c) we had buyers for both the tuna and the other business, and

    d) no one had come by asking questions.

which already showed our sales making a mystifying, nearly vertical leap during the final week of the month. Miss Onazaki entered my office and informed me that Kimura Magurobōchō had telephoned to request that I come down to Tsukiji as soon as possible. I gave the report a last wistful glance and departed.

Though it was Boys' Festival morning and the usual bundles of irises, brightly colored carp streamers, and Shōki flags had been hung in the rafters all around Tsukiji in celebration, few people at the market were smiling, and fewer still conversing. In fact, Tsukiji was quieter than I had ever heard it before, so solemn, in fact, that the holiday banners, ruffling and snapping in the sharp morning wind, were often audible over the morning's labor. The strangeness of this quiet became all the more unsettling when, as I hurried through the market, I began to feel I was being observed, not by a single individual, a tail or a trained spy, but by everyone. Everywhere I looked I caught them staring, turning away quickly when they knew they'd been caught.

They know, I thought. The sickness I had felt on seeing the first of our hybrid tuna returned. I was certain our secret had been revealed. Perhaps I'd been too visible, coming to Tsukiji now for the third time in less than a month. Or perhaps someone had finally talked. I walked faster. To my surprise, the scene at our tuna stall, despite my standing orders, seemed much the same as it had on 22 April. Several men were smoking in silence out front, and there was not a single tuna in sight. Kimura emerged from the freezer unit, followed by a very nervous Saburo. I asked Kimura if there was a problem.

As he drew near to me, he nodded and, leaning his head close to mine, said in a low voice, "Look around you, Ito-san. Slowly. Look very carefully."

I followed his directions but noticed nothing more unusual about the market than that which I have already described. When I turned back to Kimura he shook his head, signifying that I had not yet seen what he wanted me to see. Saburo was sweating heavily, wringing his hands, his own gaze flitting here and there.

I looked again over the uneasy, murmuring market around us until, finally, I spotted a very unusual man, like a plucked crane, too tall, too thin, his black suit too tight. (I assume I do not need to tell you who this man was, Minister, seeing as you sent him.) He strolled slowly down one row of stalls, then up another, buying nothing, sampling nothing, touching nothing, only pausing from time to time to ask one of the vendors a question, to which he unfailingly received a very brief answer, often only a nod, a shrug, a shake of the head. I spotted a second man in black, then a third. Our stall lay in the path of this last. The men scrutinized each stall's wares and each stall's workers with equal interest. As one of them passed a stall selling oysters, clams, and mussels, all conversation between the old man behind the counter and his two female apprentices ceased. As another approached a shrimp and prawn stall, the proprietor turned his back, quickly wrapped the pile of shrimp he had been deveining in newspaper, and slid it behind a box. The investigator seemed not to notice, but only continued on his way. Those people nearest the investigators appeared to be working the fastest, looking up every few seconds to see where the men were.

I observed the boys now, too. Certainly I'd seen them before. They had been there all along, dressed in their best for the day. But now I saw that the sons of Tsukiji's workforce played games at every corner and intersection, sparred with iris-leaf swords on stairway landings and other tactical promontories. They dodged through the sluggish crowd bouncing their balls and slinging their yo-yos, little conspirators hissing out reports to their parents on the inspectors' progress as they went.

Kimura stood loosely at attention. His face showed no emotion. The other men at our stall also watched me, waiting for orders. I looked once more at the investigators. The closest was only a few stalls away.

Of course, I could have ordered my men to do nothing. We could have made a show of cleaning up the stall, busied ourselves without exposing the truth of our situation. But I knew that these three investigators would not be the last. They would, after another half hour perhaps, return to their offices and write lengthy reports noting their observations. These reports would be passed on to other, more senior investigators who, in a month or so, would come to Tsukiji themselves and conduct an even more thorough inspection. And this would likely spawn a third and perhaps a fourth round of inspections by increasingly senior investigators until, finally, our ruse of cleaning up the stall would crumble and our operations would be exposed. The question I had to pose to myself, then, was not whether we could maintain the secret of Uokai's tuna, but what the public reaction would be to the revelation that a significant portion of the population had been consuming, in addition to the finest tuna available anywhere in the world, a shockingly enormous quantity of sashimi-grade meat derived from tiny humanoid bodies,[16] and that now we intended for them, with full understanding of the situation, to continue doing so. Better to expose ourselves with confidence and honesty, I thought, than be exposed by the press or the government like criminals.

I ordered two of our workers to fetch an uncut tuna, then told Kimura I wanted him to have the meat, all of it, ready to ship in an hour. Again, he did not falter. He gave me a short nod and went to sharpen his blade. The other men, also without questions or glances, stubbed out their cigarettes and prepared the cutting table. I looked around for Saburo, intending to have him arrange for shipment, but he had disappeared. I have not seen him since.

---

16. We had quickly discovered that, once filleted, the flesh of these bodies-within-bodies was identical in color, fat content, and texture to that of superior bluefin tuna belly, though with a perhaps somewhat purer taste, one that—according to early market research—tends to delight consumers over age sixty-five (the fastest growing demographic), who are normally wont to complain about the negative effects on taste caused by the so-called chemical corruption of the seas since their youth. Other rapidly growing groups, such as childless couples and unmarried women, have also shown a remarkable preference for the product.

Our activity attracted the attention of many of the merchants and workers in the surrounding stalls. I forced myself to look at them with a proud smirk, to hope, at least for the moment, that the sum of my positive actions would ultimately benefit Uokai, Ltd. But as more and more faces turned in our direction, first two, then three together, then six and seven at a time, until it seemed that each person's head was connected to the person's beside him, and as the swiveling of all those heads spread outward from the central point of our stall to the edges of Tsukiji, like a single great ripple across the surface of a pond, I noticed a disturbingly familiar aspect of fear and anticipation in their expressions. Familiar because I too had worn that expression, on the second day of "The Tuna Affair," before Kimura and Saburo had opened the three tuna at our feet.

In that moment Tsukiji was stilled. I turned around, looking at Tsukiji, and all of Tsukiji looked back at me.

It was true, Minister. On the morning of 5 May, all the other merchants at Tsukiji did know our situation. But they had not simply intuited it or heard about it from an informant or through rumor. They had seen the bodies themselves. They had seen them in their own stalls, in their shrimp, their crabs, their eel, their sea urchins, their lobsters, their clams, their sharks, their squid, their mackerel, their cod, their roe, in all the seafood arriving at Tsukiji over the past two weeks. All of it, or a significant part of it, carried tiny bodies inside. We had not been alone, Minister. We were only the first to test the market. This is what I saw in the faces around me. Only upon the appearance of your Ministry's investigators did we each understand that the problem was not ours alone, something to disguise with whispered code words and secret plans, but an epidemic.

I said that there was also anticipation in those faces. It was anticipation, in the final moment, perhaps wildly unreasonable, of a single healthy tuna. They wanted Kimura to halve that tuna and find only its clean, pink flesh inside, well marbled, superior, natural. And was

I not one of them, Minister, in all these ways? Indeed, I, too, would have preferred nothing better than this. I, too, hoped for a return to normalcy.

But now that I had embraced the phenomenon, now that I had authorized and committed irrevocable acts, I could not, would not, surrender the spirit of positive action so easily in the face of even this, the most desperate hope, the promise of the severest punishment. Barring a natural recovery, I thought—outwardly, as it were, as if pleading for solidarity among those thousands of faces—could we not, as an industry and a culture, simply adapt, as we have done before, and with increasing rapidity since Commodore Perry's anchorage in this very bay, to a new state of affairs? Yes, I too feared what lay inside the tuna that my men were carrying to the cutting table, but it seemed inconceivable that an entire industry should be shut down out of fear. Nations cannot eat fear.

For the moment, the faces around me conceded nothing.

The investigator nearest us had finally reached our stall, and the sound of the tuna hitting the table attracted the attention of the other two as well, who hurried over to see what was happening. Together, the three of them formed a dour cordon opposite Kimura and myself.

I ran my finger along the side of the fish. It was not the biggest bluefin I had ever seen, nor the smallest, yet it was quite beautiful, its silvery scales turning to molten gold as they reflected the sun rising over the sea of dark heads around us. I stood aside and let Kimura do his work.

The sound of the knife entering the tuna, snapping through the tight skin around its belly, accompanied by Kimura's customary exhortation as he forced the blade home, easily halving the fish, might have been the sound of Fuji awakening. There was a momentary silence that ended abruptly in the singular suck made by a sharp, perfectly balanced blade withdrawing from cold flesh. Kimura stepped back, averting his eyes so that I might be the first to see what was there. The two men who had brought the tuna to the table opened it, also turning their faces away. When I offered the Ministry's team the first look, they shook their heads in unison.

Once again, I saw a small body inside the fish. A man. His features, like the others', were both familiar and unfamiliar; his face, the face of the thousands around me. I reached down and touched his cold cheek, stroked it as my father was wont to do to me when I was a boy. I fingered the delicate structures of his fingers, fingers that in some other form, belonging to one or two or a hundred others, had touched me or been touched by me before. Legs that had run or swum beside me. Arms that had embraced me, hands that had punished me, caressed me, fed me. Would I find the same uncanny familiarity in the taste of his flesh? I wondered. His thick black hair crackled with frost, and I thought of the thick-haired boy in the photograph Sato had sent, his face blurred, by accident or design, an outrage, a living uncertainty, feeding at his mother's breast; his body, too, the product of so many others, a conglomerate like this little man's, a biological structure of knowledge, history, and experience. Yes, Minister, if the child was Sato's, there must be something of me in him as well, however insignificant, some shared physical or psychic material, just as there was something of me in this man and all the men, women, and children gathered around us. I have a son, Minister. Yes. I have a thousand.

Someone's gentle weeping disturbed the silence. The decision about what to do next seemed obvious.

I informed the inspectors that I wanted to file a report with the Ministry of Commerce.

"Yes, sir," one of them said. "Thank you, sir. Please do so immediately." Without examining the fish for themselves, they turned and left.

I returned to Uokai, Ltd. and began writing this document.

Since that time, almost two days ago, I have not left my office. Miss Onazaki is the only person with whom I have had any personal contact, though my intercourse with her has been restricted mainly to my usual receipt of newspapers and mail.[17] She has also assisted me in compiling documents for this report and making arrangements for its delivery to your Ministry. No other employee of Uokai, Ltd., including Senkai-san, has made any attempt to see or speak with me.

Concerning the facts of "The Tuna Affair," there is nothing more I can record. I await your judgment.

---

17. Miss Onazaki has also informed me of several requests by the media for interviews, but I have not responded, and do not intend to respond, to any of these. It was through the newspaper that I discovered Oshibori Saburo's traitorous fulfillment of these requests in my stead and his presumed enrichment as a result.

But what I find most curious about "The Tuna Affair," Minister, is that, according to *Asahi*, national tuna sales during the period of "The Tuna Affair," regardless of the general scandal, violent protests, marches, and otherwise significant outrage, climbed well above what they were during the whole of the preceding quarter, and even now they continue to rise. Uokai, Ltd. is claiming projected quarterly earnings of more than three times our previous best (spring 1994). If what I have done is to be called criminal, how do those who level such charges reconcile their proud pronouncements with consumers' unheeding abandon?

II.
Monogatari Monogatari

And then one day, while Yoko was out, about a year after we'd begun corresponding with S, a young Japanese arrived carrying a message written very beautifully on thin blue paper, an invitation from the old friend—for me only this time, she said—to play a writing game, like those practiced at the Heian court—a bricolage in English, an impersonation of the Empress, a plagiary perhaps, a network of tricks and allusions, words of love *to turn you on*—

And this is how it began—

Beneath the golden spring haze, Lady M and I sit in the inner courtyard, listening to the gentle fountain, to the soft, regular report of the sōzu.

My attendants wait inside, concealed behind the kichō, their whispers like the sounds of birds. Or it's the hiss of their kimonos as they shift on their thin haunches, lean forward to observe us through the just-parted silk panels, to hear whatever might pass between us—Lady M and I—to snatch a few colorful scraps from which they'll weave their filthy rumors.

Like that I am in love with a terribly jealous young woman who might wound me deeply.

But what is it?

Something has happened to the old capital.

Manners have changed.

A man came along, they say, naked, his face covered with blood. And a girl of six or seven was struck brutally by someone she had thrust off the train.

Then all the soldiers were scared away and the appearance of a wall of air on the shore at Chiba portended future disorders.

I wait and wait for the Lady to speak. Whose idea was this? Did she have something to say? Some further report for me about Shining Genji?

I had hoped to call on you immediately upon returning to Tokyo, she might begin, working up to her subject. *I'm risking my life on this project—there is no one else in the city I trust as much as you.*

But what is it? I wonder, still waiting, saying nothing.

Or maybe I asked her to come, to comfort me in this difficult time—though I would never say such a thing.

I cannot say such a thing—as if the darkness were melting on my tongue.

That's why I gave her a note for you, the night's haiku—

Someone will be murdered one of these days.

Swear to keep it a secret.

I cannot say such a thing.

My voice has left me again. So we sit. Just sit. Let us sit here, Lady M, M-san, listening to the rustling of the birds in the trees. Feel their shining black eyes upon us.

Only occasionally do I hear crows anymore, strutting along the kiri's crooked branches, dancing the Kōriyama figure—like women in antiquity, bound to give pleasure.

Almost never do I hear them.

It's just the little swallows, now, skylarks, or geese departing for the north, late again this year.

If they still haven't shown up by autumn she'll be phoning the police.

We sit so still that the world grows quiet. The Lady and I, still as stones. In a moment, the swallows will hop onto our laps and shoulders, just like in a Disney movie. I can already feel the grip of their tiny claws.

I cannot feel them.

As soon as I come here I start feeling drunk.

The buying and selling of fetuses all over Tokyo is really induced by the air pistol in my pocket.

I suppose it is only natural that their parents would dote on them, worship the whole narrative of school gear, the fiction of a life other than this.

The fact is, I would like to sell them at a low price, but I do not have the confidence.

But what is it? I wondered.

Now my head was spinning.

As in the reign of Emperor Sujin, S replied.

I smell the painted screen's ancient pigments growing dark, darker, because of my presence—my breathing—my decay. My passing, passing close, dulls the gold leaf applied by the master Tosa so long ago, dims the courtly light, the green of Lady M's spring kimono as she gazes at the radiant moon, lost in contemplation of the many duties to come.

In a certain reign, she has written on the mulberry paper before her, *someone of no very great rank, among all His Majesty's Consorts and Intimates, enjoyed exceptional favor.*

She has written: *If, in a grove,*
you discover the prettiest girl of
a good family buying and selling
fetuses, proceed by stages.

But what is it? I asked again.

A line of poetry written by Bashō.

This is a place, S wrote, *where it goes without saying that the rational is merely one system among others.*

The Emperor has changed the channel. I can almost hear it through his bedroom door.

What is it now? A disaster film?

Crowds fleeing to the far western provinces, the sea of humanity exactly following customs, pressing on toward the pileup on the eastern sea road, everything wrapped in darkness—

Perfect conditions for the tsunami.

Call it the New Japanese Novel, S wrote—

A barbaric hybrid—

*A pillow book written in English—
disordering, infecting the Japanese corpus
with the mind and language of the gaijin—
just as Ito-san tried to do.*

The most impure world of illusion, I wrote then,
a Japanese room in which anyone may justify
illicit relations on the way to total freedom.

And then, as if to explain:

That fearful moment of true awareness,
utterly physical, that cannot be recovered
by memory.

Clearly in agreement, she responded:
Obviously, one's anonymity and proper
performance enable the greatest heartlessness.

This day, I drop from golden clouds to the branch of a tall cedar.

Every room of the palace is visible from up here: ladies applying their makeup, gossiping, arranging their long combs, and daimyōs slipping back into their hakama, leaving their hairless wakashū to rest after love.

So, this is the Palace of Eternal Youth!

How handsome they all seem—

As was observed long ago, Tokyo can be light and soft to the touch in the fourth month.

A subtle, melodic charm conducive to restfulness—
A mode of life based on the art of Noh drama—
A wild ecstasy of the senses—

You shouldn't mess with me—

He's watching his television, the Emperor, watching himself bowing over the edge of a high cliff on an island far away. He is thinking: *This is a moment of great significance*. Though before, when he was actually performing this bow, he was thinking about that terrifying distance, the height of the cliff, the waves crashing against the rocks—how could he stand it?

The people who threw themselves over to avoid being captured by those beastly Americans. Those who walked over and those who were pushed, shouting *banzai* or the name of the Emperor's father, or crying *no* or *please* or *not the child*, or falling silently, or chanting *Namu Amida, Namu Amida, Namu Amida Butsu.*

Not even a birdcall could be heard.

I'll ruin everything you are—

The Emperor couldn't imagine the terror then, and even less so now, as he watches himself from the luke-warm bed, realizing that when he was thinking about that terror, he was also thinking about this moment in his bedroom, watching himself—millions of Japanese watching him, too, in this significant moment, as they did after the tsunami, declaring to themselves, and perhaps to each other, the importance of his appear-ance like this, of his goodness, his unusual accessibil-ity—so important these days, these unclean, tumultu-ous latter days of the Law, when even acquaintances rarely have good hearts anymore.

And far out in the offing, I footnoted,
the Southampton was receiving a visit
from the Emperor's boat,
edged with black fur—

A person must be rather composed, I think,
to go a year and not speak the name of happiness,
to go a year in this age of pain and not to die.

Through this narrow door, Lady M has written, *the vibrant image on the television, the Emperor once saw Yoko, that girl of whom he had heard favorable reports—strapped down by love, undoubtedly carrying a son.*

She reached gloves edged with black fur toward him, gripping his elbow, pulling him into her arms, calling the child's name over and over as she buried her face in his neck.

Results of the journey down can vary.

But what is it? I asked.

On my television, a man in a black suit and a green hard hat stands before the facility, holding up a glass of clear liquid, the visible form of invisibility.

Behind him, men in white hazmat suits stand in a row, their protective hoods thrown back, exposing their heads. Perhaps they feel they ought to keep up a show of male solidarity.

The man in the green hard hat holds up his glass, one eye cocked, as if proposing a toast. Then he drinks.

Her face has been grafted onto this other man's body.

The camera slowly zooms in to an extreme close-up recording the liquid's slow disappearance between her thin, painted lips.

Violent sadness, joy, and the potent sake were mingling within her, reminding me somehow of local safflower fields an unhappy person will never forget.

I hope it will take hours, but instead it's over.

The intimacy of the image and the lack of a cut intend to assure us that what we're seeing is absolutely real, really happening—and true.

I hadn't realized that my senses had declined so far.,

I had no awareness at all.

The Minister drinks the exploded reactor's coolant water to show that tritium is not dangerous. They have removed the cesium and the strontium, but tritium—they say it's too hard, too expensive. That it is not that dangerous. Not really. The Minister has been sent to demonstrate the coolant water's safety. Before it's released into the sea.

It's been released into the sea.

Hundreds of thousands will be getting the same nasty dose tonight.

Get used to me in you.

But perhaps it is not Lady M over there after all, beside me, slightly behind, just out of sight. Perhaps it is Shining Genji himself, disguised as the Lady. Why would he test me so?

Because he loves you—

A banal enough proposition—

On the television, a silver-haired Japanese in a dark suit stands on a cliff overlooking the ocean. He bows before casting a wreath over the edge. The camera tracks the wreath's long fall, the bright petals fluttering rapidly, terrifyingly, like the sleeves of a kimono, until it disappears amidst sharp rocks and the spray of violent waves. A crowd of men and women claps, and then the video cuts to a smiling young woman sitting behind a desk in a studio—live.

What if she were to address the reality of my buying and selling fetuses?

What if she should turn us on now to the radioactive boars of Tomioka?

It will sometimes burst
from out that cloudless sky,
like an exploding bomb
upon a dazed and sleepy town—

There was no help for him now.

*There would be no impurity in
that joy they had experienced.*

She wept endearingly, buried her face in his neck.

He has come to say goodbye, Genji-chan. It is too dangerous for him here, for us, with the Emperor so close—and he cannot bear to see me suffer, which I will, we will, surely, if the Emperor sees us together, if the Emperor returns from the television, from the edge of that cliff over which he will never fall.

It must be so.

In a moment, he will speak. Genji-chan. I feel it emerging, like a slow bubble rising to the surface. A rustle in the leaves. A slight tremor. The words almost formed, rhythm and sound that must be delivered to the neck in one stroke. Then the long time. The chrysanthemum stillness.

But it is so dangerous. Because someone is watching through the shōji, through a small hole they've made in the mulberry paper with a sharp and delicate fingernail, painted black.

Shining Genji just waiting for the spy to look away, to blink.

Delicate Genji, disguised as
the Lady M. He can feel the
eye fixated on his powdered
white neck.

He feels my longing, recalls
our last time together, in the
flowering bush clover, the
deep pleasure he gave, the
satisfaction.

I was about to come again, but I didn't.

My heart is like a ship near Okinawa
on a certain day and month—

—a moment of sharp intensity
then vanished without a trace!

A sense of intimacy developed.

*Nothing in the world would have value for them
except that experience of her on-screen.*

*Her pulsating flesh blushed.
She might have been panting.*

Nothing would be said about Yoko.

Yes, he must go! And I feel the shape of the tear in my eye, the anticipation of farewell resting just below his tongue, not even a word yet, just a sound, very small, because that is all that can be managed, all that is safe, all that is necessary, because of the Emperor, and because of the others, because of the air pistol trained on his back, on Shining Genji-chan, aiming right through him, through me—a parting that sounds just like the uguisu, who has already flown away.

I can imagine what he must have been feeling, she wrote.

She wrote: *Now is the time, M-san, the long time.*

The time to come to me. I'm risking my life on this project and there is no one in the city I trust. There is no one I trust as much as you.

She wrote: *Please do not hesitate. Do not hesitate any longer—*

III.
Backstage

The train from Ueno sat still for a long time at Naka-okachimachi—too long it seemed to him—though he'd just arrived from—

But how would he know any different?

The pair of elderly men—that girl near the door in the little baby's bonnet—the long-haired, mustached Japanese in a porkpie hat and leather bomber jacket—none of them registered any abnormality in the stoppage—

The electronic display above the door switched from Japanese to English—*Delay due to passenger injury*—

Later—on the television in his hotel room—there would be images of emergency workers standing on a train platform—pointing down at the tracks—

But now it's glistening cuts of flesh on the move—it's the chef's bark and holler—hai—dozo—o—o—arcing through the kaitenzushi—over-lit—like it's the last safe place on earth—

Where?

And when?

What time is it?

From a great height—from the most distant pole of space—just like in a science fiction film—from the fiction of a life other than this—an other's life—a fiction—

He's fallen here—dropped into this seat—feeling uncertain as drifting clouds—

It happens a lot these days—

The time?—it's on the wall—the Seiko-branded clock—it's on his phone—in his pocket—both phones—the Japanese one he's rented—and the other one—useless here otherwise—

But what time—the time of planes and stalled trains still—of in transit—of colored dishes coming down the line—carrying the only thing available at this hour—he was told—or anyway the only thing nearby—just around the corner from the hotel—in the market—

Fleshworks—the translucence of the inside—pink, red, and white—sliced, seared, broiled—wounded by three white-hatted philosophers—carefully wielding their flashing tools—laboring without cease—

The head man hollering out again—

H—ai—do—zo—o—

H—ai—do—zo—o—

Some other language at night—coming apart at its syllabic seams—its natural fissures—the sounds sounding so simple—taken to pieces in the mouth through repetition—a playful song learned in childhood—

H—ai—do—zo—o—

Blue plate rounding the curve—green plate—purple then pink—silver followed by gold filigree—a color code of value—of taste—texture—time—as in season—time to market—taken out of—some sea—taken out of time—taken to pieces—taken in—the timely code of consumption—tradition—pleasure—

In fact, she wrote—*every month according to its season—the year round—is de-lightful—*

Is it erased here—this delicate code—even here—by the machinery of the conveyor belt—the industrial-sized demand for unseasonal tastes?

Even here—in this city—in the very heart of its whirlpool heart—Tsukiji Shijō—

But how can he be sure?

He could be—this flesh could be—anywhere—

So what time is it—really—and how would he know?

Alien—*Gaijin* your only name here—you have no understanding—no taste—no sense of—no sensitivity to taste's traditions—to make distinc-tions—

Two seats away—a beautiful young Japanese—a salaryman in a black suit—watches him—eyes him more like it—eye-balls—it's what—it's him—his gaijinness in this place—the last place on earth—the most (and least) Japanese—that must make him an object of the man's regard—that makes him the subject—his gaijinness out of place—

Do you know kappa? the Japanese asks in English—smiling—gesturing to-ward the dish of kappamaki the gaijin has just lifted from the conveyor belt—just before it passed him by—as if the guy's been waiting to be noticed—been waiting for the opportunity—been spying—

A very interesting story, he says—sliding over to the seat between them—bringing along his mug of tea—introducing himself as Y—

A tall, dark beer bottle stands beside the stack of empty plates he's left behind—and an empty, sudded glass—

He draws a pink metal case from his jacket—hands over a business card—

Human Resources it says in English beneath his name—

Phone—fax—email—no company—as if that would be of no use to a gaijin—

And maybe he has a second case—for Japanese only?

His swooping mop of hair and heart-shaped face—just a boy's—a girl's—pretty and kind—

The knot of his tie—a bland silk number—sags loosely from his unbuttoned collar—a spray of purple-brown spots speckle the belly of his white shirt—slim slacks and Chelsea boots—

The gaijin hands him his own card and Y takes it with a nod—pinching it between the thumb and index fingers of both hands—reading every word softly—

M-san, he whispers—*M-san*—

M-san?

In the mirror he is still her—powdered cheeks—hands—neck—glowing from the intensity of his performance—her final departure across the hanamichi—her parting mie at the shichisan—and the few voices in the balconies shouting his Japanese name—her refusal to look back at the temple bell—a departure from tradition that will surely be criticized in tomorrow's reviews—the serpent hiss of silk—a double layer—gleaming white uchikake over blood red kitsuke—

> *And why do I paint my lips and blacken my teeth?*
> *It is because I love you, because*
> *I am happy.*

The sound of tabi on the tatami behind him—the girl's delicate scent—then the rasp of her kimono—a cicada's quiver—as she kneels to set the vase of wisteria blossoms on the low, lacquered table behind him—waiting there—kneeling—waiting for an answer—

This voice is not the one he expected—the girl's face not yet visible in the mirror—but he can imagine it—plum shaped—a gentle swell at each cheek—the careful lines of her black hair—like a frame for—

Where is Yumiko? he asks—

A pause, and then—*She's been delayed—I'll be working with you during your engagement*—

They sit for a long moment—as if listening—trying to decipher the soft exchanges between the other actors out in the passageway—their attendants and guests—quietly exuberant—

Is it all right? she asks—

What choice does he have?

He looks again into his own eyes—their strange color—they say—though not at all strange at home—in S—in America—

But here they possess an uncanny glow—here—where everything—lights—costumes—makeup—is geared toward a natural—native—darkness—

Melting on your tongue—

Here he is unnerving—sending a shudder of fear and pleasure through the other actors—through the crowd—especially them—in those moments of pure gesture—the mie—

His painted lips press together—part a little before he nods his head—a mature young woman's three-part swivel—leading with the chin—

The girl shuffles herself forward on her knees until they just touch his ass—

He imagines her face as his—grafted onto this man's body—feels again a parting in that province edged with black fur—the mirrored hall—

A slight tug as the tie at the waist of his thin cotton garment loosens—comes undone—

Do you know how a man feels when he is bound by long black hair?

Do you like Japanese girls, M-san? Y asks—the curl in his English suggesting an imminent proposition—

Do you like—Do you want—M has been asked such things before while traveling—and the answer is always yes—still—but maybe he doesn't mean it anymore the way Y does—

I'm married, he says—lifting his hand—intending to display a ring he's surprised to see is not there—slipped into his pocket again—probably—when he'd washed his hands—after they'd arrived here—a different place—a tiny drinking joint—around the corner from the kaitenzushi—a sleek little shelter in the mostly shuttered Outer Market—just five stools—the three beside theirs empty—a cool blue light behind the bar illuminating every bottle from below—every silvered surface—the bartender looking out the open door to the narrow lane—

Thunder in the distance and a gust of wind—

Or maybe he left the ring by the sink at the hotel—anyway it wouldn't preclude Y's assumption about M's interest—

Oh, she's waiting for you to come home—Y taps his phone on the bar—lighting up the time on its fractured face—*You're out so late, M-san—the trains have stopped—*

Not here, M says—*she's not—I'm—looking for a friend—*

Ah, Y nods—gazing at him as he sips his beer—*I'm so glad—*

That is—I have a friend here—I've come to find—

Yourself? Y smiles—joking—about M's age, M thinks—about Americans and their selves—

Her, M says—

You don't have her address? They can be tricky here—

*—here—*M gestures to his right—to Tokyo—

Y raises his eyebrows—leans over—as if to look beneath the stools—joking again—

The market—that is—tomorrow—she'll be—

She's a fish, Y declares—*that could be very bad for her, M-san, particularly here in the graveyard—*

A writer, M says—or maybe he would call her a journalist—a creative cryptographer—a kind of detective—he's not exactly sure who or what—

I'm risking my life on this project, she wrote—

He'd like to change the topic—not to get away—not yet—he's too awake—still lingering on another's time—but not to be the subject—not any more—

I would like to meet her—your friend—

I'm—not—

No need to be jealous, M-san—

They gaze at each other, considering—maybe laying lines—what's the punchline yet to come?—the night's ending?—or does it go on like this—M—eyes open—sinking deeper into darkness—into the Japanese—that face—

*Anyway—*M changing the tone—a release of breath—he resists—*you were going to tell me about this thing—kappa?*

Oh, Y says—*yes—yes*—does he seem a little disappointed?—disarmed?—*you know yōkai, M-san—Japanese animals?—kappa are yōkai—they live in*

117

water—look like monkeys—and turtles—both—very short—he hunches down—*like a child—with a shell—they like cucumber—so—kappamaki—*

Ozumo, the bartender growls—flexing a skinny arm—lighting a cigarette—stepping outside—

Oh yes—kappa like to wrestle—drag you under water—children mainly—but—

He looks M up and down—something else occurs to him—such a clever face—he's maneuvering them back to—

*To suck out your shirikodama, M-san—like a jewel—a pearl—the form—but your—what—the shape of your soul—your life—*Y pauses—leans in close—*up your ass—*

I don't—

Here—it's here, Y presses a fingertip against M's belly—the same spot speckled—on Y's shirt—with what—wine?—blood?—*the only way to get it out*—thrusts his other hand just past M's ear—almost knocking their heads together—smells like flesh—like some kind of flower—lips sparkling a little—that face!—and a moment of creeping anarchy—

Through your ass, Y whispers—arm resting on M's shoulder—leaning in—closer—lips almost touching—*or you suck it out—*

His cracked-up phone on the bar buzzes and Y pushes himself away to answer—in Japanese first—then shifting to English—low and intimate—*Yes—hi—hello*—as he turns his back—

Uncertain as drifting clouds—M can imagine himself now—finally—in bed—in the dark—alone—

As soon as I come here, she wrote, *I start feeling drunk—*

He stands—looking for the bartender—to pay—but Y—watching him in the mirrored niche—waves him off—

A feeling of release from my real face—

I will phone you, M-san, Y says—

Sure—and M is gone—

I see no objection—the Japanese says—*you've performed your duty with all your heart*—

Thank you desu—a voice calls from the shadows as the gaijin drifts away—

She brought a much-needed spark
to an age of extended peace–

By now, of course, Tokyo was no more than a suggestion—
fallen leaves—a warm fragrance—

Terminated beneath blocks of pure noise–

He'd sometimes imagined her—Yoko—his wife—in her former life—living in Tokyo—still married to the Japanese—taking the occasional course at Waseda—sitting by the library window one late autumn afternoon—watching the sun set over the western suburbs—

What is it?—her friend Yumiko asks—playing with her hair—as if distracted—as if it's nothing—natural—as if she isn't aware of the traces of white powder there—

She's married too—this woman—her man always coming home late—or not at all—even on weekends—working, he says—which means drinking—which is work—Yumiko explains—and bedding hostesses and secretaries—and taking it in the ass from his boss—Takahashi—for all she cares—in some cozy little condo in Shinjuku—*while I'm to stay at home and cater to his son—another generation of him—so why should I just stand by and take it?*

Nothing—it—what?—it's nothing, the woman who is not yet M's wife says—Yoko—oh Yoko—

She's thinking of the warmth of the hand of the man beside her—another gaijin—like her—but Caucasian—like M—(who's still not yet in this picture)—how the back of that hand might feel against her palm—his open palm on her—his flat wide wedding ring pressing into her thigh—her neck—as he squeezes—and their lips parting—and how they seem to become one as they suck each other's tongues—such a mysterious flavor!—a faraway place that she still recognizes—oh, it hasn't been so long really—a lovely memory of home that makes her shudder—*Hm?*

I said aren't you the lucky one—Yumiko eyes the gaijin—who just sits there—smiling—pretending to read—but she isn't talking about him—she means M's wife-to-be's not-yet-former husband—the Japanese—the executive—the workaholic—*he doesn't drink*—

There had been a boy—once—a beautiful young Japanese—M—not long after she'd arrived—who'd acted so surprised when he realized she was Sansei—or *not Japanese* as he put it—

He kept saying it—*oh, but you're not Japanese*—as if having to remind himself—as if to excuse her—

She'd been eating alone at some place—an izakaya in Shimokita—and he had a girlfriend with him—wasn't her name Yumiko, too?—who understood English—he said—but wouldn't speak—

The girlfriend shook her head when he said that—smiling—and there was something about it—that refusal—or compliance—obedience—that she didn't like—detested really—something about those two mutually positioning themselves in a hierarchy that she couldn't stomach—learned—taught—embedded in them—evidence—he might have argued—of a cultural necessity—of Japaneseness—that the American—the Sansei—could not understand—

But then—M—that face!—his sense of humor—and so much more dynamic than her husband—the first one—the Japanese—funny and fair-skinned and charming—M—impeccably styled—young—appetizing—consumable—and she could imagine—

He'd given her his card—and his Yumiko showed no response to that—just smiling—just normal—just a gesture—the girl might have told herself—just a courtesy—a kindness—her comely young M befriending a woman alone—an older, foreign woman—a lonely looking gaijin pretending she's Japanese—her Japanese hair—Japanese mask—that face—but she didn't even know how to eat, did she?

The night of the morning of the sarin gas attack—the woman who was not yet M's wife had been home alone again—her husband having already left for his office close to Tsukiji—

She hadn't gone out all day—watching the news—waiting for him to call—to check on her—but they'd been arguing again—so she didn't expect—it was that she needed more to do than—nothing—to become a full person—more than the mask—the doll—ningyō—that she'd reduced herself to—had allowed herself to be reduced to—and why?

Later—hungry—still alone—she'd walked to the little sushiya by their house—where the owner and his wife always treated her so well—not just because of her husband's reputation—or she didn't think so—but there was no way to know—

Where there was no television—of course—just a little recorded music—the sound of a koto—and the chef picking out the best of what he had—but the glistening flesh recalling what that young M had said that night—in Shimokita—about Tsukiji—*a fish graveyard*—and his impersonation of a dead tuna made them all laugh—and now she couldn't—

The flesh lived—pulsed—she was sure of it—and there was the man on the platform—the sarin victim—shown over and over—

The chef had been gracious about her refusal—*the day*—he said—she didn't understand what else—but she understood that he understood her lack of appetite—

When she got home and couldn't find M's card—the phone already in her hand—in their Western-style bedroom—she was crying—

She could imagine, she thought again that night—with M—she could still—

Or she could move her hand toward the other one—there—beside hers—in the library at Waseda—that other man's hand—lying palm down on the table—

Positive action—her husband—the Japanese—liked to say—

I'm hungry all of a sudden, she said—*shall we go?*

I thought he'd be at the office by now–

—but a strange power was driving him in the opposite direction.

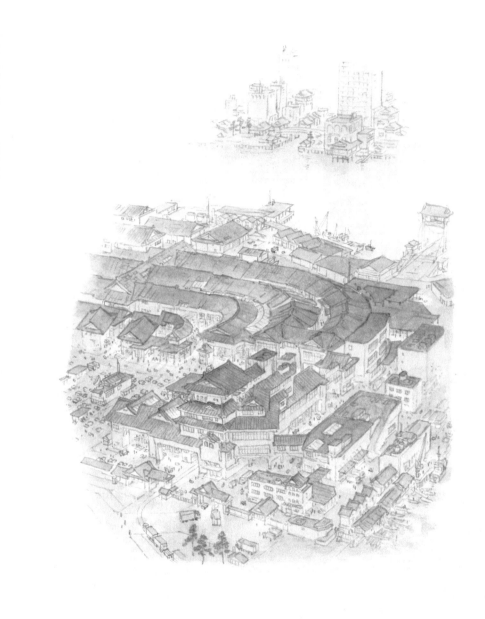

Sadohara will not get up to piss—not now—

That would require passing Amida's cubicle—the second to last in this row—to endure the stench of his panic—his unattractive, toxic cloud of anxiety about being required to work late again—(as if he were alone!)—because he's still waiting on Sadohara's pages—which Sadohara hasn't finished—of course—or really even begun—because he still can't—won't—get his head around the concept of this new show handed down from upstairs—from M-san—just a proposal really—the very thinnest of ideas—a detective story set at Tsukiji—based on a fiction M-san himself wrote some years ago—

M-san calls it a "futuro-mystery"—a rather stupid neologism rendered in typically self-important rōmaji—like something out of a vending machine—

Sadohara types: *Sadohara hasn't begun his pages because he's lazy—*

Sadohara types: *Sadohara hasn't begun his pages because he's dispirited—*

Sadohara types: *Sadohara hasn't begun his pages because—*

Well, Sadohara's got other projects in mind—

But M-san already has set and costume designers working on this travesty—

And Sadohara knows from Aika that M-san intends to cast himself in the lead—the slippery fellow—

Though why she confided this he still isn't sure—pointing the sashimi knife when she said it—as if warning him—expecting him to swear to keep it a secret—and Sadohara dodging here—there—but she kept on—kept on slashing—until—

Sadohara hasn't begun his pages because the concept is idiotic—so very ignorant—M-san's original treatment—part of the file on his desk—showing he doesn't understand a thing about Tsukiji—not really—none of the details of the market's administration—(inspectors don't show up on a Minister's request—they make random checks every day!)—of its daily operations—(there are no women handling seafood at Tsukiji!)—of all its fascinating populations—the deep villageness of it—a kind of fortress—hidden behind crumbling walls—protecting itself from the predations of the toxic city it is bound to feed—resisting the government's plans to remove it to Toyosu—loaded with benzene—so that—sure—all those men with knives might rebel—

Now that Sadohara thinks about it—in the right hands—this might produce an interesting scenario after all—

And maybe M-san's ignorance isn't so odd—he supposes—since the man lives in some western suburb and probably—like most Tokyoites—has never even been to the market—

To know Tsukiji as he does—Sadohara considers—is iki—is Edokko—everyone else—Tokyoite or no—is just a gaijin—

But Sadohara isn't so committed to M-san's demise as Aika—which is maybe why—

Though she never met M-san—only emailed and faxed with him—Aika always used to speculate that he really is a gaijin—

Sadohara grew up along the river—in Fukagawa—old shitamachi—felt as if he'd washed ashore—been discarded—

Like that first child of Izanami and Izanagi—the error—the leech they set adrift—born boneless—a pitiful mass—formless gob of spit—because she spoke too soon—spoke first, they say—that woman—Izanami—

Or like he was the Asakusa Kannon—caught in a net—drifting and providential—on the current—

Sadohara is as much a child of Suijin-sama as of either of his fathers—
the biological one—some market exec he's never known—or the adopted
one—Serizawa—the research scientist—his best and only parent really—
the man who raised him—all alone—with whom he'd frequently visited
Tsukiji in his youth—just before the stalls shut down for the day—he
and Serizawa Sensei picking out their humble purchases—(grouper—
halibut—scallops—tuna)—alongside a few adventurous housewives—
Serizawa Sensei getting friendly with the wholesalers—with the auctioneers—Serizawa Sensei asking so many questions about how buyers spot
the best fish—how they read those bodies—grade their flesh—about the
distinctions in quality between the wild caught and the farmed—(not
that that's so much an option these days with the collapse of wild fisheries)—between the foreign-born and the local—Serizawa Sensei always
looking for something more it seemed—more than consumer tips—as
though maybe he had plans to set up his own shop one day—

Or maybe that's what he'd hoped Sadohara would do—the way Serizawa Sensei was always looking at him—his son—adopted son—or who
knows what—

But instead he'd drifted away—Sadohara—drifted around—still afloat
on the waves—free-timing it—working as a stringer for *Asahi*—reporting
scraps on Tsukiji—the Outer Market—neighborhood characters—petty
criminals—the grittier bars and clubs around the city—third-rate idol
girls and weird bands—like that punk-noise trio he liked—Sumotori
Honeymoon—the guitarist and bassist wailing distortion—the strings of
their instruments grating against each other as they sucked each other's
tongues—rubbed their hard cocks together through their ripped fishnets—until the drummer leapt up—ran to the very edge of the stage—
tore off her pink, spiked surgical mask and spit on him—the wet impact
of that mass—as if she'd come right in his face—

Whatever happened to them?

So—Tsukiji—sure—

Which is why—he knows it—M-san dumped this piece of crap on him—

Sadohara hasn't begun his pages—Sadohara types—*because that's what cute little cats do*—

Because this company is okay—a regular gig—and a good thing now that Sensei, too, has gone away—abandoned him—just as his mother did—an American Sansei, they said—Pinkerton, he called her—but what did he know?

Except what he'd found on the Internet—

Orphaned again anyway—Sensei back to his secret work—underground work—shutting himself back up in a lab somewhere in the mountains—in a kind of monastery—protected by steel walls none can destroy—just like in a science fiction film—

Or so he imagines—

No word—no messages—no letters—nothing—as if he'd never been—never been his father—

So it's that time of night—a sad setting—and sad memories—

How one stuck in the shallows might evaluate the final evanescent section—the hour of death—

Though maybe not his death—Sadohara's—not tonight—

Sadohara hasn't begun his pages because he may throw himself from the balcony—as Aika did last week—as Amida will one day, too—no doubt—maybe even tonight—if Sadohara can max out that loser's anxiety—

Is this his real reason for not starting his pages—to see if he can force Amida to confront his suicidal desire?

Does that one have the guts Aika did—to make the mark of despair in the rooftop garden—sixteen floors down?

Or not?

Or maybe it'll be Yumiko—dropping the wardrobe mock-ups on Sado-hara's desk—her sad, puffy face—her depressive eyes—

I see no objection—Sadohara types—trying to look busy until she leaves—*you've performed your duty with all your heart—why don't you—*

He hovers the cursor over the send button—

Why don't you enter sorrow?

Apart from that, nothing was in any way out of the ordinary–

M-san—the night clerk looks up from his monitor—his head like a giant seed—a crooked big toe—

Gozaimasu, M mumbles—just about the best he can do—

Someone has left something—holding it out with both hands—*for you*—a small white box tied with a red ribbon—card tucked beneath the perfect bow—

Who?

The man shakes his head—*I am sorry*—*I was not here to receive it*—

His room is too warm—

M slides open the door to the balcony overlooking the alleys of the Outer Market—a couple walking hand in hand beneath the massive head of a smiling tuna—a billboard—the fish happy to give itself—to give all it has—

M undresses—turns on the television—wild boars roam the debris-strewn streets of an abandoned town—

Inside the box he finds six buns filled with sweet red bean paste—

The card is handmade—blue paper—a gold wave design—

Tomorrow, someone has written in English on the inside—delicate kana beside it—the word in Japanese, he supposes—a reading lesson—though he doesn't know what sounds belong to those symbols—how those images translate into the concept of the day following today—

Or might there be more to it—the morning—a new day—a new dawn—the rising sun?

In any case—the future—his—theirs—hers—

On the back—the sender has imprinted a kiss—a signature—vermilion-painted lips—slightly parted—an empty blue space between—

He thought he could languish unto death for her–

Born of the illicit union between dream and reality—

Was it death he was now waiting for?

Or the visitor might choose a different path—might embrace his dizzy wakefulness—call it somnambulism—play it like a game—wandering— following—walking off the flush in the cock inspired by that pretty-faced come-on—the same the woman who would become his wife had offered some time ago and far away—or maybe that, too, was just a fantasy— some humming, erotic daydream—

He might drift for a while—the neighborhood's dark current carrying him deeper into the whirlpool heart—past noir-ish, high-contrast tab- leaux of solitary diners—trysting pairs—the white-hatted itamae stand- ing by—sashimi knife in hand—past the tea shop—the kitchenware shop—dried fish and pickled goods vendors—their locked steel shutters painted with fishmonger manga—

In the courtyard of the neighborhood shrine—dedicated to Inari—the fox—guardian against the waves—the gingko's leaves quake—three carp banners rise gently into the air—a spring storm's forward breeze—black banner for father—red for mother—blue the first child—Children's Day tomorrow—or is it the next day?

An elderly man in white galoshes bows before the torii—then turns—as you do—and follows the other workers—on foot, bike, and moped— across the Tsukijigawa—down into the Inner Market—

Beside the aging wholesale shed—three box trucks idle—sides painted with samurai—herons—a dragon in flight—a couple of men offload Styrofoam containers—drivers from distant prefectures sip canned cof- fee—muttering lewd jokes to the men checking the handwritten labels against their manifests—

Fully loaded ta-rays speed back and forth across the tarmac—shuttling between distant constellations of stevedores—the shuddering beam of the single headlight illuminating a path known only to the driver—cig- arette clamped between his lips—long hair fluttering from beneath his ball cap—flying renegade—narrowly avoiding collisions—

Inside—the tightly packed stalls curve away in several rows to the south—an open fan—a bold J with its back turned to the river—

Tables and table saws—empty tanks and plastic bins—all piled up in each stall and stowed beside stacks of Styrofoam containers—for a few more hours yet—

A ta-ray rolls by—making a delivery—slowing—the driver reading the directional signs overhead—

Someone crosses between rows pulling an empty handcart—and the balding wholesaler slicing filets does not seem to notice as you pass—

You are not here—

An open box of tangled sardines on ice—

An abandoned can of green tea—

A man in a wetsuit—smoking in the shadows—

All the intimacies of the place—this secret world of work—after-hours—that Ito-san did not record in his report—would not—maybe—because—like you—he wasn't here yet—this time of day—had no need to be—was still at home—for just a little while longer—in bed—like any other man in his position—with her—

The whole of [his] professional life, he wrote—

Or maybe he never mentioned these things because they were invisible to him—so familiar—a lifetime market man—a native—a real Japanese—pure Yamato—pure Edokko—

If you believe that—

Though maybe you don't—or you will find out—find out what you believe—you will finally get to the bottom—with one foot on the stairs leading up into darkness—to the administration offices—the sprawl of shops and services—the market's hidden life—

You slip on the surgical mask—straighten your jacket—your tie—

You know what time it is—the long time has started—so you can't ease up—even if your legs feel weak—and you're leaving tracks—

M-san, they are about to say—those lips on the back of the card—the paper kiss—lips that mean to impress themselves on his—tomorrow—

He brushes them with the tip of his finger—touches her—tentative—tender—touches S—caresses the space between—the parted lips—a passage—the mirrored hall—into her whirlpool heart—edged with black fur—

On the television the man—a salaryman—black suit—black tie—looping a surgical mask around his ears—the same kind of mask M had seen others wearing at the airport—on the train—in the street—a commonplace apparently—to resist infection—pollution—the eyes of others—

He adjusts the mask—so it's a disguise and he's some kind of spy—a corporate spy—or a cop—an inspector—a detective—starting up the stairs to the wholesale shed's second floor—a world of offices—of shops and services Ito never mentioned in the report—

Finger pressed to those silent lips—

How he'd missed—misunderstood—misrepresented—the sheness of—

S—it was Yoko who'd introduced them—online—but *he/him/his*, she'd said—S an old friend reaching out—a former confidante from Japan—Tokyo—when Yoko was married still to the Japanese—sitting alone most mornings in their garden—the changing clouds—the shapes of her loneliness—

Then—one day—her ringtone—the chirping of a cricket beside the stone lamp—and then S's kind voice—a man's voice—

Maybe Ito had imagined something similar had occurred with Sato—

His near-perfect English—S asking if Yoko would be a source for an *Asahi* feature on the home life of Tsukiji's workers—everyone—from stevedores to administrators—that hidden population working while *we* all sleep—the men—mostly men—who feed us—*us*, he said—who provide the stock for groceries—restaurant kitchens—pantries—who dissipate—evaporate—in sunlight—

Like vampires, he joked—tried to—perhaps sensing her reticence—

We—*us*—had he meant to include her—the gaijin—the Sansei?

He knew this in advance, she thought—knew how she must have felt— knew to speak English—

I see, she said—*and I'm queen of the crypt?*

That reined in his horse—

But even then she imagined burying her face in his neck—

A small bird flew out from beneath the deep eaves—

Petals began to rain down—

He will not be especially pleased, she said—imagining that face listening to her voice—*Yes*, she said—*okay*—

Cut to: a nearby stall, where a man—just a silhouette—in a glistening wetsuit—(as if he's just emerged from beneath the dock—having scuttled someone's fishing boat—set a small, weighted body adrift)—has been observing the detective—

He flips open his cell phone—enters a number—the screen's light illuminating the line of his cheek—a close-up—the glowing cherry of his cigarette obscuring his face—its heat intensifying as he takes a drag— waits for someone to answer—his sharp and delicate fingernails painted black—the tattooed tentacle of an octopus curling across the back of his hand—

And later—he'd agreed—S—to give her private language lessons—writing lessons—though M always suspected he'd also been a lover—the way Yoko talked about him sometimes—their outings around Tokyo—overnight trips even—to Nikkō and Kyoto—though why should this matter to him now—to her husband now—M?

The way she turned her face when she talked about his friendship—how S had helped her through the separation—the divorce—the transfer of the child—how he had advised her—restored confidence—her body pressed against his, M thought—*as if rediscovering*—she began to say—*what lay in me*—as her hand emerged from the darkness—as they sucked each other's tongues—seemed to become one—to touch him—*but also the shape of*—M—how could he stand it—*something brand new*—

The woman who emerged unsteadily from the mirror—gloves edged with black fur—just as he'd first seen her—

I see no objection, the man in the wetsuit says—then snaps his phone shut—

Five steps and he's at the top of the stairs—

The detective looks back—sees he's leaving tracks—but he can't ease up—

The warmth of S's hand on hers—guiding her brush through the seven strokes of *man*—the three strokes of *woman*—the two lying together— one beside the other—too close and tentative—on mulberry paper—language—flawed but legible—

He gets angry when I call his daughter in Hiroshima–

This girl has unusual strength—what did she say her name was?—Yoko?—pressing her thin forearm into him—like a steel tool—kneading through the right side of his upper back—contouring every rib—pressing him deep—deeper into the cushion—forcing a sigh—

He hadn't realized how deeply tangled he'd become—perverse, he thinks—

Was it the long flight?—This business with his wife?—How they'd left it—before his departure?

And then the strange phone calls he'd been receiving since he arrived—from a serious young man—speaking resonant nonsense—half of it erotic innuendo—the rest apocalyptic prediction—

M would have called the police if he didn't admire the creep's poetry so much—

Last night, for example—

Someone will be murdered one of these days, he'd declared—*swear to keep it a secret*—

M nodded in his dark hotel room—as if in agreement—and neither of them spoke for a while—

On the television—the detective was disappearing up the concrete stairs—into the market's ceiling—as if he were being swallowed—sucked up into a mouth—just his legs now—his shoes—then gone—

M never spoke when the man called—except for the first time—demanding to know who it was on the line—how he'd gotten this number—M's Japanese phone—

Last night—left confused once again—a bit terrified—but intrigued, too—uncertain whether to hang up or to hold on—should he call the police?—someone at the theater?—or was this just a harmless madman after all?—a bored shut-in?—someone truly dangerous?

Some ultraright thug maybe—part of an organization that sees the engagement of a gaijin by a prominent theater in Tokyo as threatening—a pollution of the Japanese stage—

He'd been made aware of such possibilities when the offer was extended—threats phoned and faxed to the money men upstairs—his agent told him—executives who would have to convince investors—who had reason to fear disruptions—public embarrassment—even the possibility of assassination—

Seriously?

Or maybe the guy on the phone was simply a too-avid admirer—

A moment of static and then M could hear him breathing—calm—even—then a clicking sound—like keys on a computer keyboard—a little flourish—not like the caller was composing anything—but maybe searching the web—pulling up information—on M maybe—or images of people tied up—kinbaku style—something to inspire his weird monologue—

Hiroshima is Paradise, he said at last—then hung up—

Now she's punishing his left side—that tool-like arm—balancing him—inside and out—and he's breathing himself into it—the pressure—loosening himself—drifting into that space she's making—so vast and pacific—

No doubt, the caller had said on another night—*the central market has already been named for the buying and selling of fetuses*—

Now that will inspire introspection—

Waiting—like fine spirits—
brings the most divine sort of torture—

In this rare atmosphere of congeniality–
I received reliable information
on the timing and scale of the earthquake–

To the left of each door—on both sides of the long hallway—a bright yellow plaque bears the office number—embossed in black—

On the right—a narrow, vertically oriented window provides those inside a clear view of those passing by—and vice versa—

In there—the same tableau is repeated over and over—an office lady behind a desk—staring at her computer screen—typing an email maybe—or entering the previous day's sales data—a man in a black suit standing nearby—or seated on the leather settee—chatting with another man—wearing an identical suit—pointing to a page of an open ledger laid between them on the Noguchi coffee table—

But it's just you in the hallway—your steady pace—the dry impact of your steps amplified by the bare concrete floor—no other bodies to muffle the sound—the walk you're now consciously modeling on Lee Marvin's at the beginning of John Boorman's *Point Blank*—the man named Walker—back from the dead—walking toward—her—intercut with—her—his traitorous wife—waking up alone—making herself up in the mirror—reflected to infinity by the mirrors at the hair salon—all those reflections of her beauty reflecting oddly—reflecting Walker's rage-warped memory—his perverse desire—not for love—

Revenge—

But here there's only the echoing of your shoes—and the faint sound of a koto—

That face you can only imagine—

And you are the mirror—

Any one of those men in the offices could be you—could have been—if only you'd been born Japanese—

But here you are—out here—walking—like Walker—still searching—for the number she gave you—Room 2082—

And no one looks up—no one notices you—their reflection—passing—

And then there's your phone buzzing in your pocket—the Japanese phone—

Who could it be? Who else has this number?

Maybe you should be at your office by now—but a strange power—

And you're still drifting—touring these sordid corridors—drawn on by an irresistible current—into deep—deeper water—into the whirlpool heart—

Because you're sure of the number—the directions she gave you—because there is no one else in the city you trust as much as her—S—

So you've memorized the map—just a list of intersections and turns—a sequence of maneuvers that will lead you there—Room 2082—

Arriving not too soon—but before it's too late—

S stripped bare and bound up shrimp-style by The Pure Land Group—in a secret back room—a Japanese room—hidden behind a panel in the tokonoma—the interrogation is already underway—her punishment—

For turning you on—

Oh, Yoko! Just what the hell is Serizawa working on?

Turn left at the cafeteria—the jumpsuited stevedores there chatting in groups—reading the paper—magazines—their phones—the floor seems to suck at your shoes—but don't ease up—turn left into the transecting corridor—identical to the first in every way—the vertical windows—the office ladies—the black suits of the salarymen—except that at the next intersection there's a bookstore selling antique erotic woodcuts—an electronics shop—a tea shop—a Mizuho bank branch—each with shallow eaves decorating their false fronts—the trompe l'oeil sky painted on the ceiling reddening now into artificial morning—a little in advance of the real one outside—where it's overcast with a light drizzle—just as predicted—out there—where Tsukiji is hurtling toward the final half of its day—

Don't stop—

Keep on until you reach the knife shop—a sashimi knife in the window—the blade etched with cherry blossoms—turn right—take the next left—the second right—yes—now you're deep inside—

Keep on—keep on—until the blue light of the artificial dawn illuminates the display windows of the Mitsukoshi branch—where an android model catwalking in front of the video screen showing petals raining down looks so like her—your wife—the last time—the same black leather skirt and oyster blouse—the same green silk scarf and bug-eyed sunglasses—hiding her eyes as she approached the mirrored doors of the terminal—her reflection there your last image of her—not her actual face—because she didn't look back—

How sad for you—

Beautiful women are so cold they say—one feels them to be the source of all wanting—

Oh, but don't stop, M-san—don't stop now—come—you've almost arrived—please don't leave me now—like this—come—

Filled with the most intense feelings of sorrow and regret—

Even your impeccable reasoning—
with which you went to so much trouble—
completely collapses in the middle of this dream—

A slit in the body—passage for the experienced hand—her father's hand—

Entrance—or exit—

Are they male or female—these fish—bellies sliced open—gills cut out with a short sword—on the deck of whatever ship landed them—in whatever sea—harvested—fins and tails sliced away—sometimes also heads—

Bodies sheathed in frost—mist curling around them—arranged orderly across the auction floor—these tuna—

Buyers huddle with auctioneers—her father explains—inquiring about each one's provenance—asking for a little more—a hint—a tip—any signs of trouble—

Reaching into that wound—that unctuous slit—to touch the fat—examining the surface for flaws—signs of a damaging struggle—hints of the internal burn that turns the thick flesh soft—watery—white—excavating the tail end with his hand tool—his single-clawed tekagi—

He extracts a chunk of flesh—rolls it between thumb and forefinger—performing for her—shines his flashlight on her face to make her smile—then on the meat—pops the scrap in his mouth—makes some notes about color—oil—translucence—

The girl—ten—maybe eleven—wearing galoshes like everyone else—standing in the wet—scuffing through blood—pink galoshes—free from school because it's Friday—the day before Children's Day—

Because he wants her to see this—or she wants to see this—or they have no choice—no other option—because school is out—and her mother is—where?

At work—home—away—gone—gone back to America—lost—just another body—

Or—

They wanted her—the girl—to see—to show her these bodies—to show her what takes her father away while she's sleeping—the source—or one source—of their food—of her home—her comfort—of all that she knows—all they share as a family—all her life—for as long as she remembers—since before she was born—the watery—the bloody—

Could she know this?—the moment of her beginning?

To imagine home as a body—this maimed, half-frozen body on the floor—at her feet—to equate them—for the first time—this is that—

The dirty—the sordid—this world of buying and selling—*this is home*, she thinks—*this fish—this body—this is my jacket—this fish—my galoshes—doll—bed—book—this is me—us—*

Around noon is when it gives him back—this world—when it relinquishes him—back into light—into air—his bedtime the same as hers—even earlier—for now—*for a few more years*, he says—*before you're up all night with me—with a tutor—cramming—*

She doesn't want to think about it—

To imagine herself inside—at home in there—this fish—as it had been—at the beginning—

Is it male or female—this slit-open body?

Working her way out—into air—burrowing—oh—eating her way through the soft flesh—its translucence—otoro—otoro—the snap of its skin—opening its scaled surface for her—from the inside—

To imagine herself in another—as she was in Mother—the watery world—the bloody—

Little fish, they say they called her—before she was born—

Did he see her—see her coming—naked—face almost entirely covered with blood?

Or was he here—at Tsukiji—one hand inside—

Can she—could she remember it—if she tried?—that memory of being born—stored somewhere in her—in her flesh—a little fish—

Now here in pink galoshes—standing again in water and blood—

What her father knows about them—these bodies—how he sees them—as potential and defect—kilos of valuable flesh—translucent—the thing that precedes food—the perfect fish—the perfect shape—the perfect—flashing through his head—information in flesh—his strange power—strange sight—

And how he looks at her sometimes—little fish—

But also taste and texture—that fish in him—that flesh—in every part—is him—and her, too—this is that—*that flesh is mine*—that translucence—the underneath—

This room will be empty, he says—every body sold in seconds—gone—wheeled away—then back again tomorrow—but new—the same but different—kilos and kilos of flesh—

Still his little fish—for a while longer—for a few more years—until she loses her tail, he says—becomes fully herself—a young woman—ippan-jin—an ordinary person—an outsider—like any other visitor—gaijin, he calls that woman—gaikokujin—not his but another man's—not Tsuki-ji's—not anymore—

She doesn't want to think about it—

Handbells ringing—the auctioneers step onto their footstools chanting *what'll you pay what'll you pay*—each in his own manner—the buyers—her father—making laconic gestures—the same every day—index finger and thumb—claw—fist—wagging hand—

The winning bid written right on the tuna's skin—in black ink—as if on mulberry paper—

More than ten years ago Sadohara saw that girl—

Back in early Heisei—the day before Children's Day—the first time— he's sure—that he saw himself in another—as another—not dressed in her skin—as if it were a costume—but in the very flesh—a young woman emerging unsteadily—

This is that—

And then catching his father's dark eye—Serizawa Sensei watching him watching the girl—as if making the same calculations—connecting the same points with the same lines—as if completing some complex equation in his head—

My mask was flawless—

Gloves edged with black fur reaching through the open window—

M's wife had introduced them—M and S—over email—just a memory of hers then—S—until then—a man—a Japanese she once knew—who'd helped her through a sad time—an itinerant language worker—*a freetimer*, he said—left behind with everything else—silently circling Tokyo's whirlpool heart—part-time journalist—translator—calligraphy teacher—just a memory—

Until he reached out again—through the open window—found her online—then rematerialized as paper and ink—as a manuscript sent to the accounting firm—to her office in America—for her eyes only—almost without comment—just *I thought you'd be interested*—and *translation mine*—his note—handwritten in an artless, horizontal hiragana—signed with his stamp in red—like blood—

The two of them—M and his wife—conferred about it—the manuscript—a report—as if it was authentic—a fiction, yes, but also not, she said—not exactly—because its author—narrator—sounded so much—too much like—the husband—the first—the Japanese—more than M could have known—

As the craving for a child suddenly reasserted itself—

But also not—not like that husband—not exactly—

In the garden she told M that he—S—knew—had known—that husband well enough to recreate him—to perform him that way—as text—

Because S was a performer, too, she said—laying aside her magazine—had even trained in Kabuki for a while—playing koyaku—white-faced children—just one kid in the crowd—and always an outsider—a gaijin—not being a member of proper Kabuki family—

Sometimes, she said—taking a sip—he seemed so outside—she'd wondered if he was really Japanese—

But, no—S wrote—it wasn't his—this manuscript—in fact, he'd received it anonymously—without any invitation—on his doorstep one evening—a hand emerging from the darkness to ring his doorbell—leaving behind a stack of handwritten pages—bound with a branch of wisteria blossoms—

An orphan, he called it—filthy nosed—a pigtailed child—an interloper—an especially beautiful child—slightly blurred—with black, unfocused eyes—

The craving for a child—

But what is it? she wanted to know—pulling the string on her white, silk pajamas—

A fake, S insisted—his responses addressed to them both now—M and his wife—*a fraud,* he called it—*speaking Japanese strangely*—as if it had studied—like her—a few classes at Waseda—just enough to pass—for a moment—before one might say *oh, but you're not really Japanese*—just enough—and maybe just a bit more—

Their mouths seemed to become one as they sucked each other's tongues—M and his wife—the craving—*positive action,* he called it—joking—

But really, she said—emerging from the shower—*he really did say that*—the first one—the Japanese—*please stop*—

Because as months passed unproductively—she began to worry that they—that she—that her body was toxic—

As if, she said—as they waited for the doctor—*in fulfillment of a curse—tatari—the revenge of unwanted things improperly disposed*—

S's orphan comment really wound her up, M thought—of course he knew all about it—the child—the first—the only—or as much as she would tell—

That child—back then—hers—with a Japanese—with S, M speculated—pouring coffee—though he couldn't be sure—

The only—the only child she might have—might have had—she worried—waiting in traffic—the sun in her Japanese—in her Sansei eyes—that child she'd left behind—with the utmost loving care—on the day observed long ago as the Kamo lustration—

Hers alone to make, the Japanese husband had demurred—that choice—any choice having to do with the future of *her* child—because—just like the husband of the manuscript—the handwritten husband—her first had denied his participation—*not mine, certainly!*

So it had to be S—the author—didn't it?—who else?

And maybe he'd been right, M considered—the first one—the Japanese—because she never confirmed otherwise—not to him—

They sucked each other's tongues—he imagined it in the dark—his wife and S—

Because she could do that then—leave everything behind—because she did it—leaving the Japanese husband for a second time—because she'd gone back to him first—as she'd promised—back to Japan—as the wife in the report said she would—then left again—like Amaterasu hiding herself, she'd thought—rising gently into the air—a wave of darkness engulfing Tokyo below—the child—K—left behind—asleep in the lap of her aging friend and neighbor—the research scientist Serizawa—having never married—with no one at all otherwise to tend his ashes—the child K—left behind to grow up motherless—but still loved—in the Japanese way—

Because she would be dead to them all—to Japan—would kill that self and begin again—

The woman was not defenseless—

Except this shadow of sadness—

Their mouths seemed to become one—M and S—S and M's wife—as he buried his face in her neck—

Your gestures must be more gentle, S wrote to him—to M alone—out there in America—in the dark—because finally M's wife had refused to participate any further—leaving the mystery to them—because she didn't care any longer who it was reaching out in that manuscript—reaching out for her—because she knew who it was—as the craving for a child suddenly reasserted itself—

And how was it that they'd come to write each other about these things, M considered—just the two of them—M and his wife's lover—former lover—about M's wife—about the child K—about M and his wife's troubles—their lack of productivity—

You need to appear more than just tender and gentle, S wrote—

Or was it the Kabuki they were discussing now—S's training—not just as koyaku—but as an onnagata—male performing as female—what S had learned from his mentor—emerging unsteadily from the mirror—a woman—

You must switch off your own body—know the scent of her skin—the taste of her—you must portray her inner feelings—

Until it was that body M believed in when he buried his face in her neck—not just S's text on the screen—not just language—but S's fingertips tapping the keyboard—S's fingers—S's Japanese body—the woman emerging—her voice—her slim neck—those same white fingers that would point to the red bean paste buns—that would lift the blue card to her painted lips—on the day M was to arrive—those soft fingers that reached toward him some nights in the months between—in the darkness—M's wife asleep beside him—taking him in hand—lips pressed against his ear—*Are we having a party or not?*

Her face in the mirror—

She will not be especially pleased, M responded—

It's just the way we are—

Her words on the screen—gloves edged with black fur reaching through the open window—

M's legs feeling weak—but he can't ease up—

Dancing the way one's only love should do—

S—and—

I ought to let you know, she wrote, *that I myself am due to bear your child—*

I recognized something in the mirror–

It had happened!

Why does her arrival at Tsukiji station—that shaggy-headed kid nodding off on a bench—remind her not of that day at the auction with her father—all that profit and loss—but the time she took them both at once—the guitarist in her cunt—the bassist up her ass—or was it the other way around?—or it was both, wasn't it?—one then the other?—then waking again—after all night—all three of them out of their heads—the real Sumotori Honeymoon—a pleasure of such magnitude it should have leveled Tokyo—

Pressed between them after—just a pause—spent and a little frightened—her small body—feeling slick and nasty—tucked inside—disposable—like a wounded doll—while the boys went on and sucked each other's tongues—seeming to become one—both their heartbeats in her ears—she held on to them anyway—all she had then—to them both—imagining herself as their baby—making some kind of noise—

Growing hard again inside her—they pushed her away—took each other for a while—face-to-face—like women bound to give pleasure—

How things ended she couldn't even remember—

But feeling them again—feeling sick for the loss—every one—

And stopping herself on the Metro stairs as the crowd moves past—bodies brushing against her—the sea of humanity—exactly following customs—lost in contemplation of the many duties to come—

The tail and hindquarters of a rat vanishing—

That once—Sadohara had discovered Aika in the breakroom—blouse off—draped over the back of a chair—bra straps slipped from her white shoulders—like a peasant girl—weeping beside a stream in a historical film—

She hadn't left the office for two days straight—

It wasn't the first time—or the longest—

The cheap shampoo she used bloomed with artificial strawberries—the rushing water—her slim hands working their way down the black column of her hair—

Sadohara stood in the doorway—

The curve of her back—the movement of muscle and bone under her skin—spine—like stones in a stream—scapula—rib—curve of breast—the small nest of hair as she raised her arm—

That took his breath—

She didn't seem shocked or embarrassed when she finally noticed him—half Korean, he'd been told—so not Japanese either—though it wasn't obvious—not to him—*so beautiful*, he thought again—admiring her as if he were looking in a mirror—

What do you want? she asked—shutting the water off—

I was going to make some tea, he said—*would you like some?*

Get out, she commanded—*I'll be done in a minute*—

Later, the room still smelled like that—fake strawberries—a little girl's scent—not that of the thirtyish, unmarried woman he'd been watching—hunched over the sink—though at the time—that scent—that body—they seemed to make sense together—

Loser dog, the other guys called her—and all the unattached ladies on staff they were too ashamed or afraid of to ask out—an office—a whole building full of distances—of reticence—

She'd left no evidence behind—only a small tangle of hair in the drain—

Sadohara extracted it with some chopsticks—wrapped it in a paper towel—took it back to his desk—let it dry there—laid out like a pile of seaweed behind his computer monitor—

They'd been reprimanded a month before for clogging the breakroom sink—but no one knew the source then—or, anyway, he hadn't—

How had she gotten away with it?—and for how long?—long enough to clog the sink—

They'd been made to apologize to the janitorial staff—

Why didn't she use the ladies' room?—he looked in there—confirmed they were the same as the men's—the sinks—too small—maybe smaller—to discourage this kind of behavior—

Everyone else must have known—all the other guys—but kept it to themselves because they figured he'd have no interest—*someone like him*—

Sadohara following another path—total freedom—appearing as a boy or a girl—depending on his mood—it didn't mean he didn't desire—the one—the other—both at once—

Later that day she sent him a cruel email—a critique of his scenario about Manjiro—the fisherman—the castaway—one of the first Japanese to emigrate to America—by accident—exiled from still-double-bolted Japan by the swift Kuroshio—rescued from shipwreck by an

American whaler—risking execution when he returned contaminated—then helping the West to pick that lock—

She'd cc'd M-san—like she hated him—Sadohara—wanted him gone—

Then she'd thrown herself off the balcony—into the garden—

And he wanted to imagine it as an act of love—

The tangle of hair—once dry—did not achieve the same softness—the
same sheen he'd expected—some residue left it tacky—

He threw it in the trash—pulled it out—took it to the men's room and
washed it again—worked it through his fingers into individual strands—

Back at his desk—he wrapped the clean hair tight around his pinky—
making the tip bulge—imagined it around his neck—tugged harder as
he read her last message again—again—searching for hope—something
to take from her criticism—his face turning red—then blue—

He could not understand women, she said—

She probably wasn't wrong—

The long waves of her hair spreading around her as she fell—eyes
shut—like his—as if already asleep—growing longer and longer—envel-
oping her—braiding together—turning to feathers—

There was a crow at a nearby temple, he'd been told—known to dive at
lady joggers and women pushing strollers—

They saw you take me into your mouth–

THE WIFE:

(lying on her side, eyes closed)

He only imagined me asleep in the lukewarm bed—

The girl—playing the husband—crosses the room too quickly—without grace—she's no professional after all—not yet—but with some natural subtlety she pauses—as the script directs—starts to glance back—then changes her mind and exits—

THE WIFE:

(eyes snapping open)

Men do stupid things sometimes—

The girl kneels by the dressing table and softly recites the chorus's lines—

CHORUS:

Five steps and he was at the top of the stairs—

When necessary she'll rise to mime the other roles—the Japanese ex-husband, the journalist, the lover, the son—

THE WIFE:

He was leaving tracks, but he couldn't ease up—

CHORUS:

Who could have spread sand in the hall?

M has rolled onto his back—knees bent—hands clasped to his groin—shoulders pinned to the floor—raising his hips toward the ceiling—slow and pulsing—lowering—rising again—again—again—

CHORUS:

With a black-nailed finger, she urged him—
With a black-nailed finger, she eclipsed that one, too—
With a black-nailed finger, she brought herself to bloom—as the

lover used to do—

like Flowers of Edo—

M shudders—spasms—eases down onto his back—knees splaying out—loose and lazy—satisfied—a drifting mood—a moment of associative reverie playing over his powdered face—before he realizes he's been drawn into a whirlpool—

Flipping over onto his belly—as if tossed by an invisible hand—and the girl rises to her knees—concerned he may actually be suffering an attack of some kind—that face!—he really seems to be shrinking—going down—through the floor—but she eases back again—relieved—maybe delighted—as his awful expression evolves—revealing traces of love—a somewhat softer anguish—something like nostalgia—perhaps—for an alternate world—as called for in the script—

A woman—not a girl—or feeling a girl—made to feel a girl—trying to recover—restart her adulthood—

And still a mother—mother to an orphan—the child she abandoned—gave as a gift—though she's never—she cannot—embrace this act as generosity—or as failure—not exactly—not necessity either—though at the time she knew how—knew it was best—best for herself—to be cold—but how could she—having held him in her arms?

She extends a quivering arm—all the weight of that offense—lifting her head—allowing it to turn slowly from left to right—

The fullness of her sadness disturbs every space in her—its intense physical presence—a constitutional pain—present at the surface as the white powder covering her entire body—

At the limit of her reach—finding no one—nothing but a wall of air—she brings the arm back—slowly—like a retraction—a withering—to

take it all back—curling in—toward her heart—fingertips—wrist—elbow returning to her—head turning right to left—resting her face on the
tatami for a moment—in the dust—before beginning again—reaching
out—the sequence repeating over and over—like waves coming ashore—

And soon the girl is past observing him—past wondering if this is how
M-san intends to perform the scene—or if he's simply rehearsing the
moment—perfecting it before moving on—before linking it to the next
gesture—

She is drifting—no longer admiring his subtlety—but meditating on the
part of her that remains unconvinced—that cannot be deceived—not
by him—

Because she really knows the pain of that surrender—

Because a doll may have been the best she could do—

The best she could do to honor it—

This is that—

The child she had not had—

The mizuko she named—

The name she will never say—

The doll she carried to Ueno Park—to Kiyomizu temple—to the ningyō kuyō—

Because she could not then imagine another future for herself—

Not this one either—

Her mizuko—she says—whispers—*I'm sorry*—*I'm sorry*—

Because she may have—

Because she may have been—

Because their future was Los Angeles—to rage in torn fishnets at the Troubadour—the Whisky—the Roxy—

To surf—to smoke on the beach—to drift—drifting clouds—the desert night—and she could imagine—

Because she may have loved them—S—M—guitar and bass—and also K—and yes Y—but less so—or what did it matter?

Because the band—

Because she would be as she wanted—would be Sumotori Honeymoon—with S—with M—

And how they fought—fought her—each other—when she told them—cursed her for carelessness—

But it wasn't her—wasn't just her—

Because S and M had gone on with themselves—never spoken to her again—

I'm sorry—I'm sorry—

Up the temple steps with a doll she'd just bought—

That heaviness of the body—the lightness of the unused doll—

Of water and blood—of silent liquid—of the mizuko—

One does not need to be dazzling like an alien from another star—

But Ito never mentioned Suijin-sama—Tsukiji's patron deity—his tiny shrine right here in the market—across from the loading docks—at the end of a row of shops and restaurants—

Strange, isn't it, S had wondered—because wouldn't Ito—so dedicated to tradition—a market man—*the whole of my professional life*—have been inclined to stop here before returning to his office on that twenty-first day of the fourth month in early Heisei?

Might he not have purified his hands and mouth at the temizuya—dropped the largest coin he had in the offering box—rung the bell—clapped his hands—woken the god and asked that he never see again what he'd just been shown—that *defective tuna*—that *monster*—a catastrophe not just for his company but for Tsukiji—the geographic heart—the narrative heart of his imagined Edo-Tokyo—

So disturbing—so disgusting a sight—think of it!

Wouldn't Ito-san desire a god's help then—even if he wasn't—as you call it—a believer?

No, not a joke—as Ito had first thought—but maybe a crime—*his word*—or a warning—perhaps—the job of the monster—all monsters—to show—

Or maybe, S wrote—*she was the first instance of some wronged spirit's revenge— what we call tatari*—

I reflected on the effect they might have
on the crowds milling around outside—

Worrying about the life to come—

But when he arrives—it's already too late—

The key he'd been given—wrapped in thin blue paper with wisteria blossoms—opened the door—Room 2082—just as the note had said it would—a room of shelves crammed tight with books on fish—market histories—poetry—novels—manga—an old wooden desk and a shabby central table—covered with more volumes—scattered with newspapers and industry magazines—

In the back room—the Japanese room—he passed through the tokono-ma—through the secret door—into the mirrored hall—where she—where S—

But there's nothing—no one—just the largest tuna the detective has ever seen—lying on its side on the bare concrete floor—lit by a single dangling bulb—light reflecting harshly on the lacquer-like sheen—the defrosting fish's damp surface—

Its belly sliced open—revealing fine meat—the severed crescent of its tail shoved up into the gap where its gills once were—a commonplace at Tsukiji—though in this context it seems like a message—a threat of humiliation—

So—they'd expected him!

But what about S?

Had they really brought her here—as she'd predicted—or was it all a setup?

Had she been in on it?

He turns in place—scanning his reflections—as if one might move inde-pendently of him—as if they—someone—might be back there—behind any one of them—watching—but what else can he do?—he can't ease up—the long time has started—

He circles the fish—the floor seeming to suck at the soles of his shoes—his legs feel weak—who would sacrifice such an enormous—enormously profitable—specimen like this?

Only a clan—of course—a corporate conspiracy—a diverse criminal syndicate with money and influence—and nothing to lose—

Peering into the fish's upturned milky eye—he sees nothing unusual—

The enormous body—wide enough—long enough to hold a human—carefully folded—knees hugged to chest—as infants once were—the archaeologists say—back in the Jōmon period—arranged for burial in clay jars—

As the notion blossoms—that characteristic crease—familiar to his fans—deepens between his thick eyebrows and he drops to all fours—peering into the fish's open mouth—trying to illuminate that abyss with the faint light of his cell phone—just barely revealing inside—another, duller sheen—some unnatural object—a solid mass—edged with black fur—

Or—hair?

The mime of grief he begins now is exquisite—very Japanese—stamping feet and delicate hand gestures—he extracts a fan from his inside coat pocket—leaving nothing to the imagination but the sound of a koto—

After a few minutes—the interpreter is about to step in—but I stop him—

Let him finish, I say—*he's exploring*—

Do whatever it is you people do, I'd told the interpreter to tell the actor earlier—*here is your motivation*—

And then I recited the line I'd been worrying in my head ever since you last wrote—the line you signed off with: *All they'll find in the locker at Kamiyachō is fear and whale meat*—

The same line spoken—recited—by the young man whose call had awakened me last night—my first night in Tokyo—before the line went dead—my Japanese phone—

Who was he and how had he gotten the number?—unless you—

The interpreter stared at me as he translated—as if maybe I'd misspoken—but the actor accepted my direction without alarm—the crease between his eyebrows suggesting he'd even been anticipating this—as if the line was some kind of code I'd been meant to deliver to him—a code that might permit my entry into—

Or that he—the actor—was part of this same conspiracy into which I'd been groping my way all along—during those nights online—corresponding with you—sinking deeper and deeper into your whirlpool heart—

On the flight over—I'd dreamt us going down in dark—into the black Pacific—

How did I survive?

And her—my wife—her flight went down, too—the two of us taking up residence together again—like Izanami and Izanagi—on a fragment of charred fuselage—planting gardens across an archipelago of flotsam caught in the Pacific gyre—cultivating radioactive fish and seedlings to feed the New Japan we'd create through our ritualized rutting—a race in our own likenesses—quite literally—each face—each body—only fractionally different from ours—so that it was near impossible to tell one from—

And there—even I—somehow—have become Japanese—

While she looks as she always has—like one of them—

From beneath a red parasol—she speaks and I understand every word about the process of fermenting indigo leaves into the sukomo she's made to dye our happis—

Or that was a film I was—the Japanese next to me was—watching— Kaoru—an accountant making his home in Portland now—headed home to some western suburb for the first time in six years—one historical scenario after another he watched—samurai and kamikaze—General Nogi and Empress Jingū—all the way from LAX to—

Or it was the film I was writing—

Or it's this one—

What do you think, the interpreter whispers—as the detective continues—

I think I was hoping I'd spot her—maybe tomorrow—at the arrivals hall—or later—in the market crowd—wearing the same green scarf and bug-eyed sunglasses—my surgical mask and salaryman suit disguise enough that I might follow her unnoticed to your rendezvous—

Is it the Café Diamond, maybe—where you first met—by the Kaminarimon?

Or why not your apartment—crowded with novels—your translations of Mishima and Kawabata and Abe—all your Japanese books—every one a translation—that gives you away—as one of us—a gaijin after all—

Wasn't it you—you that wrote: *You are destined to meet yourself waiting for the traveler?*

You—you fraud—

Wasn't it you that turned me on?

The young Japanese plunges an awl precisely through the eye—fixing the head to the gore-slick board—

The wounded body—still powerful—even more so in its paroxysm of pain and terror—continues to flail—rage—until the man clamps it down with his free hand—slits it open lengthwise—pulls out its guts and spine—slices off the head—leaving a long, spade-shaped filet—

In Osaka they commit seppuku, Ito says with a smile, as if beginning a joke—*in Edo—Tsukiji—shitamachi—we still respect the belly—open the eel from the back*—

He's revised himself—the narrator—the Japanese—shaved his head—all that wonderful hair—the *great rolling wave—poised to break*—gone now—gone out with some long-ago tide—sucked out to sea—leaving a dark shadow in its place—the hint of a shoal or a sunken wreck—an underwater hideaway—some mad scientist's secret lab—just like in a science fiction film—

Is that respect, M wonders—*a courtesy to the eel—or is it superstition—a fear of destiny—as if one worries that—if they cut* his *belly then*—

The bald, brown dome and black suit—the black mandarin collar—give him the appearance of some kind of priest—

Like a bat that passes for a bird, she used to say—

It's preferable to what they do in Osaka, Ito shrugs—stepping aside for a man with a handcart loaded with tuna—*superstition, tradition, there's no difference here, M-san—Tsukiji lives on both—Tsukiji is both*—

But how can he be trusted?

His English is perfect—toneless—without qualities—the first thing that might give him away—that might break the spell of his Japanese face—which seems not so different from M's own—as if—as Barthes says—*he's been Japanned*—and aged, too—

I may be fortunate, M considers, *to be—then—so at peace as he seems now—*

Shall we walk, Ito asks—already underway past a stall of shrimp and prawns—another selling live crabs—restless under a pile of sawdust— *you've been wanting to see it all for yourself—*

I'm supposed to meet—she said—

S-san—yes—I know—and you will—I think—find her—but not here—at the old house—

Whose?

*You'll need to take the Metro—like this—*and he begins to recite a complex list of lines and stations from memory—as if reciting a prayer—*Namu Amida—Namu Amida—Namu Amida Butsu*—the two of them reciting and repeating—back and forth—until M has the sequence down too—

Nothing looks as it did the night before—all these rudimentary shops— (too spare and packed too close together for the privacy Ito claimed he and his men had in the report)—shut down then—mostly empty—only one merchant up late—or early—slicing fish by lamplight—

Much of the night's activity had been concentrated in the auction pits— where they were already laying out the lots of tuna—the headless—the mostly whole—

Now—in the late morning—as sales have slackened—a number of the men stand around chatting—drinking tea—canned coffee—

A woman in one stall's kiosk-like office seems to be catching up on the accounting—leafing through slips of paper—recording the day's sales—

It seems to me now more like theater than a machine, Ito says—*like Noh and Kabu-ki—like so many things—traditional things—Tsukiji has its patterns—kata—passed down from master to apprentice—these same cuts for over four hundred years—since Mogoemon arrived with the shogun and all the Tsukudajima boys—*

M spots a middle-aged Japanese leading what looks like a small tour group of gaijin down from upstairs—probably from the live fish or uni auction—on the next row over a Japanese camera crew is interviewing a man specializing in boiled octopus—

Every cut has its own knife, Ito says—*representing some long ago and also present customer's need or desire—essential maybe—Japanese, that is—expressing our taste—but also individual desires—impulsive and unknowable—*

He sounds tenuous—speculative—not exactly—and yet—

The need paired with the tool, M picks up the thought—*the knife—the tool also always a weapon—a potential present elsewhere, of course—*

The mallet, Ito offers—*the awl—*

But two sides of one blade—a kind of mirror that cleaves—

I'm so glad you understand—

Plastic tubs and cardboard boxes overflow with remnants—fins and severed heads—a pan of blood—

Everything so whimsical and imprecise, M-san—how the buyer interprets the auctioneer's information—reads a future in the shape and feel of a body—like pulling a fortune at Sensō-ji—even the prices at the sushiya—based moment by moment on the chef's impression of quality—his impression of the customer, too—all of it as uncertain as drifting clouds—such a strange effervescence—

Frozen bodies laid side by side—fed through table saws—hacked at with axes—

The market, perhaps, as he says—but Ito more so—and M cannot deny his imagination—*one must learn to breathe it to survive*—that whirlpool heart—*writhing and unrestrainable*—a body in ecstasy—a site of transformation into—S—lips parting to speak—

M-san, Ito sighs—*just look*—

There—a man with a sleek, sliver chonmage—using a white cloth to wipe down an exquisite section of tuna—a meter-long pink wedge—half a meter wide at its apex—a truly beautiful object—

He's as gentle as if he were caressing a lover—her luminous interior—her taste—like a second tongue—sliding across M's tongue—unable to speak—

He refolds the cloth—begins again—whispering as he works—complimenting her maybe—praising and encouraging her—*my darling*—apologizing for her suffering—the way one's only love should do—promising a joy to come—

Here, every wish can seem intense and fragile—
like tears of sympathy—
or the name of the author—

It is the story of Izanami and Izanagi updated—a contemporary Noh play set in a future in which the crisis of Japan's dwindling population has reached its final stage—

Loser dogs—herbivore men—wakashū—otaku—beautiful young joshi and danshi—all the unproductive androgynes—uncertain as drifting clouds—meeting up every evening after work—like water birds on the bay of Naniwa—to dance the Kōriyama figure in a most impure world of illusion—a whole underground network of Japanese rooms in which anyone may justify illicit relations on the way to total freedom—

There will be so much sex—erotic innovation unknown since the Tokugawa period—

Except they're all impotent!

They don't even produce sperm or eggs anymore—bodies born toxic to them—not that anyone's looking to reproduce anyway—because of the responsibility—and relationships really are so much trouble—

And no one wants a lab-grown clone—or to appropriate other animals as hosts—for what?—to gestate the wretched material deposited by previous generations?—dark liquid and failed grains—marigolds on a quilt of mud and fallen leaves—

Japan 2082—

Reticence is no longer a social condition but a physical mutation—

The mind and mixed emotions have finally changed the body—

And the most beautiful thing will be the final passing—the last generation—

Petals, they call themselves—petals raining down to the sound of a koto—

But one old doctor—(modeled after—well, we'll call him Tomotoki)—may prevent disaster with his secret government-sponsored experiments—propagating genetically altered tuna at his underwater lab—extensive as Ueno station—constructed on a former seaweed and uni plantation near Dàlián—

M—a salaryman working in telecom—and S—an office lady at a major bank—have been chosen as the project's first subjects—lured into consuming—for one month—something called Y—a fish substitute, they say—the men in white coats—

Lured also into falling in love—or maybe that was easier than it seemed—

Except M is an impostor!—an administrator at one of Japan's few remaining fish wholesalers—and Tomotoki's adopted younger brother—both of them—(along with a ring of corrupt government officials and twenty-one important members of the Imperial Court—collectively calling themselves The Pure Land Group)—positioned to make billions and billions—enough to buy every square meter of Tokyo—

If the doctor's fish induce S to bear one healthy child—

Because the enhanced tuna—*Codename: Yamato*—(Sadohara's title for this scenario)—not only turns you on and makes your body more accommodating through repeated doses—but it is tasty!—and its flesh is so compliant it can simulate anything—sea eel and horse mackerel—premium Ohkost crab and Alaskan salmon—creating conditions for a sushi boom—(all those new babies will need to eat!)—and for the revival of traditional foodways for the first time since an exploded reactor killed off the local fish stock—(already near collapse)—and contaminated the world's remaining wild fisheries—(same)—making the country a singular pariah—subsequently incurring harsh economic sanctions for attempting—again and again without success—to manipulate the farmed fish market—and for poaching in the few remaining clean sanctuaries—essentially returning us—with great popular support—to a pre-Meiji policy of closure—sakoku—(so traditional costumes and sets can be used—reducing costs)—

This time we'll remain closed—at least for a while—until—

And thanks to Yamato it won't be only the wealthiest corporate daimyōs anymore who can afford to eat at even the shabbiest local sushiya—

Meanwhile—M-san—Tomotoki Sensei—and The Pure Land Group intend to leverage their wealth—the anticipated population boom—nationalist sentiment inspired by the humiliation of the foreign sanctions—to orchestrate a new imperial era—

The Maguro Restoration—

She had hesitated because she was unsure of the time—

A souvenir that originally had been no one–

From a great height—from the most distant pole of space—

She must have fallen asleep on the way from—

Was it she who had directed the cab—or had someone instructed the driver to bring her here—the white-gloved man leaning on his car now—across the street—smoking—waiting on her—

But that face!—to see it again—the face of a child—her child—the only face—darkened and worn—the once smooth surface pitted and—just a single red thread around the neck—all that remains of the new bib and knit hat the statue—Jizō—had worn when she last saw it—purchased it—more than twenty years—how she'd left it when she left him—them—the only face—the only face she'd known since—

Until that beautiful young Japanese in her office—the man his company sent—the importers based in Vegas—though it was his age more than anything—more than his face—that suggested—that he was the same age as—

Because how could she know—how could she know how that child—her child—had turned out—and what Serizawa was up to now—having kept their agreement—to forget and to obscure—to deceive—

But wasn't it possible—possible that he—the Japanese from Vegas—was—that he might be—but—

I'm not what I appear, he'd said—when he noticed her staring—hands at his side—though he wasn't there to behave that way—to be apologetic for anything—sent from Vegas to answer her accounting firm's questions—as tersely as possible—not to explain or excuse irregularities—as she would discover—

That is, he said—*I'm older than I look*—bowing his head—confessing with a smile—he would concede nothing—*though I admit I may use a little makeup*—his company was promoting research, that's all—*just a little concealer to smooth things out, if you understand*—research that would ensure a continued—and affordable—supply of tuna to American sushiyas for years to come—and yes—she could see it then—moving closer—close enough that he'd smell the scent of cherry blossom—feel her almost touching him—and maybe there was a bit of color on his lips, too—pale pink and sparkling—a trace of white powder at the margin of his crow-black hair—the great wave of it—the physical craving suddenly reasserting itself—emerging unsteadily from the mirror—his face in hers—their mouths seeming to become one—and she could imagine—

But *oh, you're not Japanese*—even then—as if he'd known from the moment he entered—even before that—had expected it—despite her Japanese name—her near lack of an accent—her face—except that sprinkle of pigment across the bridge of her Japanese nose—what she'd always thought had been the first sign—giving her away as a gaijin—the flaw in her mask—

So—

Let's not waste any more of your time, Y-san, she said then—switching to English—and the interrogation began—about his company's unusual investments in a certain product—the R&D done by The Pure Land Group—(weird name)—based in Tokyo—with a facility in Dàlián—(why China?)—the interrogation into that central mystery—that whirlpool heart of the account—referred to in memos and ledgers only as Y—

Dolls—needles—computer chips—tea whisks—eyeglasses—ancestors—all the things that have served you well—but had now become surplus—*that is the purpose of kuyō*, S had told her then—*a ritual of farewell*—*an honoring*—*a pacification*—not that either of them believed in tatari—but the ritual itself—the act of atonement—would ease her conscience, he said—until—maybe—when she was ready—there might be another child—the expense of the little statue—the remainder of that body—that regret—that she would never see again—worth it—perhaps—even if she didn't believe—so long as the concept could give her peace—

And had it?

A Japanese in a black suit has approached her taxi driver—asked him for a light maybe—or no—they're just talking—the salaryman wearing a surgical mask—

The object—the statue—that face—left behind—like something of great value—a pair of shoes—no—like a ring—a wedding ring—engraved with dates and initials—irreplaceable—that one would never not regret—

So S—so Serizawa—all of them had to know—she would be back for it someday—

When they lied—she and S—and told the priest performing the ceremony she'd had a miscarriage—

A lie—as if it wasn't a miscarriage—as if she hadn't somehow felt it that way—as if she didn't know what miscarriage really felt like—though didn't she?

This is was that feeling—she'd thought—as the priest chanted—her performance totally authentic—

A man and a woman—husband and wife, she supposes—father and mother—greet another statue a few feet away—speaking to it in low, coaxing voices—*How are you?—What have you been up to?—Do you like this?*—placing a toy car at their Jizō's feet—bowing again—standing silent—hands at their sides—reflecting maybe on the child's response—the alternative future—perhaps already arrived—underway—in which that mizuko emerges again from the watery world—to find happiness—at last—with others—or maybe returns to them—these two—because they're ready now—or she is—and this man is the man to be a father—

For the good of the boy—S had advised—*for all of us*—*to have your chance again at freedom*—how he'd organized the details so quickly—through his connections, he said—as if he'd done it before—the child's transfer to Serizawa—but why had she obeyed—again—the illusion—the illusion that she controlled her situation—even now—her legs feel weak—

I'm sorry, she whispers to the statue—*I'm sorry*—*I'm sorry*—as she'd left the neighbor's home—K quiet in the man's arms—and,then—for her—only this—this face—the weight of its stone—its immobility—

Until he'd reached out—as if from the depths of the ocean—

The salaryman is gone and her taxi driver checks his watch—where does he have to be?—where does he have to deliver her?

The scent of cedar incense smoldering in a brazier drifts over the garden wall—the Japanese on the other side standing in a line to make their prayers at the Ankokuden—wafting smoke onto themselves as if it were water catching in the folds of their clothes—

Namu Amida Butsu, they mutter—*Namu Amida*—*Namu Amida*—*Namu Amida Butsu*—

The mother pours tea into three small cups from a bright blue thermos—places one beside the toy car—

I take refuge in Amida Buddha—

In the golden-walled Daiden—Hōnen Shōnin—his brightly painted likeness—sits smiling in the deepening shadows—

There are various ways of escaping from the world of illusion, the founder of Jōdo-shū instructed Shigehira—about to be executed for destroying the temples of Nara—*but in these unclean, tumultuous latter days of the Law*—the *best one is to recite the name of the Amida Buddha*—

The great bonshō has sounded—the monks are closing the east-facing doors—

Perhaps he's sorry he couldn't be more help defeating Gojira–

When she finally got through to him—they agreed to meet in Asakusa—

I have to buy a present for someone who's going away, he explained—

Man or woman?

Does it matter?

I—I don't think so—

No—

And Yumiko?

I'll be alone—

I hope nothing's happened—it was only a week after the sarin gas attack—

Why would you say that?—she could tell he was smiling—

They met that afternoon outside Tawaramachi Station—she took a cab—still too afraid of the Metro—

But it's as safe as it will ever be, he said—just like everyone else had—

He'd taken the Ginza line—in fact—following the attackers' route in reverse—

They greeted each other with polite bows—just like associates—before walking on to Kappabashi-dori—gazing into a few shop windows— pausing at a sidewalk display to let her inspect the china—

I kept my distance—far enough so that she wouldn't spot me—my reflection in the glass—his rival—and glad I'd thought to buy it—the surgical mask that seemed—almost—to make me Japanese—

But all this was just play—they both knew it—a digression—evidence of the difficulty she felt—trying to find her way free—uncertain as drifting clouds—she felt slightly embarrassed among what felt like thousands of flashing eyes looking down upon her—her head was spinning—

But that face!—framed by long forelocks—like the wings of a crow—

And he showed no impatience—his smile a mirror of her own—reminding her of starting again—to die—to have died—like the man on the platform that the news had shown over and over—to start again—death was supposed to liberate those people—that's what the group's guru told them—but that was murder—hers would be voluntary—her choice—

They stopped for ice cream—red bean paste for her—peach for him—

In early Meiji, he said—*Japanese refused to drink milk—makes you smell like gaijin*—

And taste, she said—

The choice to live as she wished—to be that independent—

Was it so hard to remember what it was like to be unattached—like Yumiko—his Yumiko—in love—

But she was no Yumiko—she wouldn't have allowed him to betray her this way—if his Yumiko was anything like her—he wouldn't be here right now—in Asakusa—with her—playing this coy game—in advance of—

He would've been ashamed to meet up with another woman—she would have made him ashamed—she's sure he would have hated loving her—she would have made him hate that—hate her—he wouldn't have called it love anyway—that's not a word for him—and yet he would have stayed with her—because there could be nothing else—there would be no one else—nothing he could do—it would be her or nothing—just like the old sewamono she'd been reading at the library—research, she'd joked—love suicides—double suicide—the Japanese knew everything about this—much more than her—because they had the courage to end it in blood—

He might still—she might push him there—

And she might feel bad wounding him—but that is how it has to be—

At the knife maker's—the blades were displayed by width and shape in descending lengths—laid out on angled shelves—beneath recessed lights that accentuated the rippling patterns on the gleaming surfaces—the watermark—two waves of steel coming together in the forge—the hard and the soft—

The squared nose is for vegetables, he explained—*curved for the all-purpose santoku—an axe shape for soba and udon—for fish, a leaf or spade shape—an angled wedge for eel—this one for paring—that one for boning—*

Every cut has its own knife, she said—again a little embarrassed by what she didn't know—what she couldn't have known—(she and her husband had a woman in to cook for them three or four times a week)—what she didn't want or need to know—

Embarrassed for feeling so young with him—so free—

Mirrors that cleave, she was thinking—looking over all those shimmering blades—

He was ten years younger—at least—his smooth face appearing in the blade beside hers—a kid—maybe that was what made her think she could own him—

M smiled and rocked on his heels—

He knew a lot about knives for a junior associate in Human Resources—

I suppose you would call it a hobby—he said—*otaku*—jabbing his chest with his thumb—*I have a rather large collection, actually*—*though I don't cook*—because he wanted no smells lingering in his apartment—his excuse for always meeting elsewhere—*and I'm very slim*—*I don't eat much*—

No surprise—then—that the gift seemed more decorative than useful—a sashimi knife with cherry blossoms etched on the blade—set in a velvet-lined box—hinoki—Japanese cedar—with brass clasps—

The elderly owner—Katagiri—attended them for more than an hour—already knew M by name—and they bowed deeply once the decision was made—

He would have walked on past the statue of a golden kappa—but she insisted—

His business completed—she knew his expectations—about what should come next—hers, too—and theirs—the men in white coats—

I had already observed them consume their doses as instructed—

Tonight would be the first time—how many more she wouldn't speculate—but it would rain later—and she would enjoy what was left of the light—she would please herself—

She wanted him in the photo—

It's just a marketing campaign for the district, he said—*all these banners with the innocent, kawaii character*—*the real kappa is a rather nasty creature*—*not like this fellow*—*isn't he handsome?*

One more, she said—

A couple of girls in pigtails took photos with their phones—and he smiled for them, too—the one with pink hair and a big polka-dotted bow stepping in with him—grabbing him around the waist—holding up

a peace sign—him, too—yes—he could be a television star, she thought—
or one of those dewy, androgynous pop idols—more than your average
salaryman anyway—but the girls didn't ask for an autograph—just the
photo and directions—

They drag children into the water and drown them, he said as they walked
on—*suck their life out their ass*—she pulled a disgusted face that made him
laugh—and she sensed his scorn—inherently masculine—despite his
seeming frailty—his fey surface—a young man's scorn that would become an older man's—her husband's—he would use her—whisper to
her on the phone—learn all he could from her willingness—her curios-
ity—entertain her for a while—experience the gaijin—then move on—

(Oh yes—he knew that she wasn't Japanese—and maybe the others
did, too—Tomotoki—The Pure Land Group—so typical that such men
would allow a catastrophic error to occur so that one might be satisfied
two or three times—how could they stand it?—such a strange example
of greed makes one hesitate, doesn't it?)

Anyway she didn't care—she wanted him—and she'd take something
from him as well—

Shirikodama, you called it?

All she could take—all there was that would remake her—remake
her world—because this wasn't going to be a question anymore of
him *or* her—there would only be the one who didn't continue and the
one who did—the one consuming the other—then moving on without
sentimentality—

Later—in the precincts of Sensō-ji—she drew her fortune: *You are destined
to meet yourself waiting for the traveler*—

But what does it mean?

That's up to you—his white hand emerging from the darkness—touching her hair—

They made their prayers to Kannon—then strolled back through the ancient gates—the mostly shuttered stalls of Nakamise—

Later still—he led her by the hand through the shadows—which was his?—to that lane behind Hanayashiki—

Five steps and they were at the top of the stairs—

Her legs felt weak—but she couldn't ease up—

As soon as I come here, he said—lowering his face—*I start feeling drunk*—

She nodded—buried her face in his neck as petals rained down—

She said: *There is no one else in the city I trust as much as you*—

There would be no impurity in that joy they had experienced—

The directions seemed to presume that he would be followed—

Buy a *Sports Hochi*—get on at Tsukiji station—the first car of the north-bound train—sit by the door—

Press the emergency stop button at Hatchōbori and get off—

Walk to Kodenmacho—

Get on the train—the third car—northbound—put down the paper at Aki-habara and continue on to Ueno—put on the wig and the dark glasses—

Buy a copy of *Nikkei* and take a taxi to Shinjuku—Marunouchi Line—the fifth car—all the way to the end—Ikebukuro—then all the way back—Shinjuku—and back again toward Ikebukuro—exit at Kokkai-gijidomae—

Buy a *Shimbun Akahata* as you switch to the Chiyoda northbound—first car—as far as Sendagi—Exit 1—

And then wait for him to arrive in Sudo Park—there—in the shadow of the Benzaiten temple—

Who?

You'll know—but do not attempt to approach—

Ito pours the tea—exhales quietly—leans back from the counter—the leaf-shaped dish before him empty—

There's no television in the sushiya—of course—just a little recorded music—the sound of a koto—

After the squid—the horse mackerel—the fatty tuna—

After the fresh-caught clam and octopus—the bay scallop—the salmon roe—the sea eel—

This—this translucent chunk of flesh before M—seems the worst possible ending—

Its appearance suggests fish—but its color—something else—a deep red streak angled through its center—fanning out—thick and dark along one edge—flecks of pigment just beneath the surface—burst capillaries—perhaps evidence of its final struggle—or—

Or something like the freckles on his wife's shoulders—the lightly speckled bridge of her nose—what always gave her away, she said—though they both knew it was more—

But the itamae is watching—expectant—so—

The taste of it is water—unremarkable—near tasteless—not so bad—until a hint of bitterness—salt and mud—and even before he begins to chew M feels a peculiar tingling on his tongue—spreading around his mouth as heat might—a tightening—like a response to tartness—the billowing pleasure of umami—in his chest and arms—the tips of his fingers—his hips—his toes—as if his whole body is contained in his tongue—is—a tongue—

If I turn you on now, S wrote—yes—something like that—

If I turn you on now, it will be a major breakthrough!

A caress of soft textures—gloves edged with black fur working up into him—his erection—a dance along the rectum—the far-off shrill of an insect—

That summer, someone was saying—

Never has he tasted such total freedom—

That summer, someone is saying—*I had my first taste of weakness in some time*—

The woman at the other end of the sushi counter—the onnagata—

Mangiku, Ito called her—as if M might know the name—her voice and powdered face so unnatural—but also a delight here—delicate and supreme—black eyes—crimson lips—suspended in that white absence—the void of her lying, clean-shaven face—the space between her lips—that parting—as if taking him between them—the whole erogenous surface—

Her mannerisms familiar to M—as if it was his real wife sitting there beside that other man—the Japanese—his back to them all evening—

Every day—she false whispers—singing it—*filled with unclean deeds too numerous to count*—

Her eyes on M—so that the man—the Japanese—her husband he must be—finally begins to turn—to look back at—the manly curve of his face—

And the feeling of release from his own—

To arrange oneself—like the iris—
upright but approaching repose—

Whoever it was had a word concerning the fallen leaves–

The irresolvable remainder—
The empty shell at the bottom of the bowl—

A slow horse crossing the pasture—
the cuckoo's song—the touch of her hand—

M-chan she called it—the mizuko—as she told it stories—

He sometimes—or sometimes *she*—as the mood suited—

While washing dishes—folding laundry—on her way to the theater—the university—

But always *you*—

You—tonight—in Ueno Park—on the shore of Shinobazu Pond—

Tonight—a tale she's been reading in her American literature course—about life aboard the whaling ship *Pequod*—her Japanese masts—in that Japanese sea—

How her father's Tsukiji—auction floors covered with bodies—day after day—has shaped her understanding of Melville-san's commercial world—of Ishmael-san's belief in the immortality of the whale—his naïve underestimation of the long time—of the ingenuities—the hunger—of men—

How the work of the *Pequod* seems to her not so different—even now—from that of the fleets of purse seiners and long-liners—freezer trawlers—factory ships—at sea for months—and more—hunting what remains—enough bodies to make the endless voyage pay—longer and longer—crews sleeping in bellies of death and blood and violent machines—freeze and wet and mediocre food—wild castaways—unfit for any society but that—out there—at the most distant pole of space—nights alone with other men—one's only love—

And she thinks of him—screaming drunk as they used to—standing on the deck—tonight—at the edge—in the north Atlantic—beneath the haloed moon—rain gear slick—hardening to a coat of ice—as if—

The sea—she tells M-chan—*a mystery still—like yours—the infinite—the unwarped, primal world of nonbeing—your preexistence*—which she imagines not as the barren riverbed of theology—ruled by punishing demons—but now—thanks to Melville-san—as *a thousand leagues of blue—that serene ocean rolling eastwards—each drop of it a new thing—yet to come alive—sweet mystery and awful stirrings—you in among them all—M-chan—dreaming—dreaming still—billions and billions of you—outnumbering the fish—so many—and rising up—higher than Mount Sumeru—tonight maybe—finally—into one great wave—already on the threshold—to suck us all out to sea—*

To begin again—

Please forgive me—

When M—the bassist—had started to email her—just over a year ago—she was surprised to discover that he—the thinnest—the most girlish of them—had taken a job on one of those brute ships—the freezer trawler *Pequod*—

Perhaps you've met him then, she said to M-chan—*in the spray—on his lip—he's licked you up—tasted you—salt—himself—me—a memory—your father—that one—or—the other—*

But M has never mentioned S—or the days of the band—

Oh, she's changed, the girl thought—

Photos of himself on board a Chinese ship—an American—a Norwegian—with shipmates—friends, she supposed—each time—though why not more than that—he might still—as the mood suited—

Not recognizing him—at first—through the black mask of facial hair—

Photos of a red-faced Japanese—a blue-eyed gaijin—drinking cans and cans of American beer—a men's club in Newfoundland—Nantucket—his body no longer his own in the embrace of some hideous, blonde kappa—topless—big breasted and dazed—

It wasn't a matter of his *growing up*, was it?—something more like emerging—coming to shore—coming up out of—

He sent videos, too—of a day's catch, once—a purse seiner in the Pacific—the tuna still fighting and flexing on the deck—one of them rigid—stilled in a fatal crescent—*flipped-up ass* her father called it—their massive bodies made pathetic and terrible in the wide slick of blood—the hunched men wandering among them—gilling them with short swords—slicing open their bellies—wounds she'd observed at the market—but had never seen inflicted before—

She couldn't watch it all—the video—not even once—her sense of disgust changed now—grown in her—like a living thing—mizuko—it had changed—that—what she couldn't watch—or eat—any longer—

But otherwise?—

What she could do?—what she was capable of?

Life at the theater had been revealing—in that mirror she was Yoritomo—

Anyway—she'd gone veggie—and maybe how she responded to the video—the massacre—had led him to introspection—

There must be another way, she wrote—*farms—yes—bluefin raised from eggs—circling wild in pens—but maybe—also—also—what?—*

The dark sea—the dark waves—

And *oh, she's changed*, he must have thought—contemplating his desire to know—examining this—as if it were an object outside of him—his desire to reconcile—with her—with—it—mizuko—to escape—maybe—the whirlpool heart of the ocean—to die to that and begin again—as she'd done—as he'd done, too—awaking on a ship somewhere—but now again—in need of another—just one more—another image change—

But—

I must be a miserable bricolage of error, M wrote—one of his old lyrics—*I hope to call on you immediately upon returning to Tokyo—*

But—

The little wavelets of Shinobazu tickling her calves—thick mud sucking at her soles—

Perhaps we're all too late, she thinks—

Past it—that point—in the abyss—

One lotus flower blooms on the surface—

Her legs feel weak—

Is that a kappa's claw at my ankle?—or is it you, Mizuko-chan?

What if tonight could be Tokyo's last?

The sashimi knife in her hand—blade etched with cherry blossoms—

Positive action—

Sometimes—it seems—a man
must leave you for the form
of the pretty woman he's taken on—

What S wanted was to love her—or to know her—by which he meant understand—her—understand why—why he was who—what—he was—the
parts of her—in him—

How love might wrap itself around the organs and penetrate—tear the
body—tear the self—apart—reform it—with fragments of the other—
entwine—substitute—bone for bone—and flesh for—this as that—every
piece nearly the same—giving no sign you are anything other than—

Her—

To remake himself not as son but as lover—not as husband but as rival—not as himself but as—

Her—

No—really—that—and all of that—and—

To love—to be—be inside—again—this woman—his mother—who was
not Japanese—not exactly—

Which made him—not—either

To love her after what she had done—which was abandon him—

Like a lover—

Was to authenticate him—falsely—as Japanese—to confer a false provenance—the only child of old Tomotoki—the slippery fellow—

Though what did it matter?

A synthetic monster they've put together—

To be her mirror was what he wanted—to show him herself her—

Choked with tears—lamenting the fact that he had not been born

Japanese—

Though what did it matter?

Only the feel—the taste—the sensation of Japaneseness—like faded silk—he thought—the remnants of an old kimono—clotted with blood—

Except at the heart—the whirlpool heart of this project—this human market he was risking his life on—being authentic—pure Yamato—was—was the only—the most—the central element—that purity—if they were all to survive—

Or that was the story—

And he was a lie—

Reaching gloves edged with black fur through the open window—toward her—her slim, white neck—wrapped in a green silk scarf—a souvenir of Tokyo—

What S wanted was to understand how—how this woman—how love wrapped around—entailed—

And how could he stand it?

That is—he admired it—after all—what she'd done—positive action—felt he must do the same—whatever that means—to die and begin again—in America—because the central market had already been named—for the buying and selling of fetuses—

The removal of a hundred eggs from a certain well-known woman—

That is—he—his—whatever it is that's next—that's coming—the future—is a synthetic monster—put together in China—bound to emerge from the sacred mirror—followed immediately by another—by another—almost impossible to tell one from the next—

The Japan of Tomorrow—

Then her husband's novel fades to black as a call comes in—replaced on the screen by a phone number she doesn't recognize—

But who else would have it?

She answers anyway because she's supposed to—because she's just been sitting here waiting for contact—from who?—who knows?—only it's what he wrote on the thin blue paper—*sit there—wait—you will know—*

But she doesn't—know—

It's just a man's voice asking for her husband—or anyway for a man with her husband's gaijin name—M—

Gomen nasai, she says—*I think you have the wrong number—*

Ah, I'm sorry, he says—continuing—as he began—in English—his only language—*I meant you—Mrs.—correct?*

Will she be that?—will she continue?—she thinks maybe she has a choice—except something—his breathing—says he knows exactly who he's speaking to—who she must be—must continue to be—unless—

Yoko, she says—*Who is this?*

A friend, he says—*over here—to your right—see?—near the exchange window—*

A couple who've just exited through the mirrored doors of the passport area greet the family that's come to meet them—mother—father—boy and girl—the women look like sisters—twins—hard to tell one from the other—

Do you see—

Not yet—

The little group moves toward the escalator—revealing behind—some-one—a young Japanese in a black suit and tie—holding his cell phone so she can't see his mouth—mirrored sunglasses similar to hers—his long hair a little shaggy—maybe a wig—obscuring his face even more—and he's turned sort of obliquely—looking out the terminal's glass wall at the bus and taxi lane—his left hand rising casually—twice—as if by habit—just above his waist—

Is that really him?—or—she glances behind her—could it be someone else on the line—this man some kind of decoy for whoever else is watch-ing—

That is—the voice doesn't sound Japanese—

That's me, he says—*you saw me*—

Okay—

The question is not that—because that—the Japaneseness of the con-tact—was not specified—

The question is does she trust him—meaning is this clean—professional?

If he came into her office with a theory about those Japanese in Vegas—about what Serizawa is really up to—would she be prepared to listen?—this is her position now—a senior partner at the accounting firm—with powers of determination—what she's earned for herself—in spite of—as a result of—everything—

Go outside—get in the first taxi—the driver knows where—

Where?

He knows—

But I have something—

He knows—

But—

Go! Now!

And he hangs up—the man by the exchange window holding his phone at his side—turning his back—but still looking out at the street—

She stands with her small bag—three blouses—a pair of jeans—cropped pants—a skirt—underwear—toiletries—enough for a few days—maybe a week—long enough to determine if she'll ever return—or if she and S will—if she and S can—and M—

He seems to feel her coming toward him—maybe sees her in his peripheral vision—from behind his dark glasses—so he turns and walks away—quite quickly—past the onigiri and bento and phone rental stalls—half-glancing over his shoulder then—still never giving her more than a profile—only the hint of red lips—almost exactly like hers—through the long crow-black hair—almost exactly the same as—

Excuse me—she's not quite shouting at him—*excuse me*—

The phone at his ear—he's calling her again—

Excuse me, she answers—

You were told, the voice says—*not to approach*—

It's the same voice—except the aural mise-en-scène is not correct—not the voice that's incorrect—but the sound around it—not the sound of a man talking while walking fast through an airport—

But I will not be told, she says—slowing—letting the decoy—the actor—go—*I will not be told*—*we agreed on that*—

Please, Yoko, her husband says—*there's no time*—

More Japanese are emerging from the customs area behind her now—Chinese, too—a few Europeans—Koreans—an even smaller fraction of international others—

It was uncomfortable—the flight—you know this—I'd like to go—to change—couldn't we just meet there?

I've got another appointment—you know this—just go on to the taxi and we'll see each other tomorrow—

Even so—she appreciates the indulgence in his voice—knows he's trying—trying to make it all work out—

All right, she says—*but please*—

She slips out the automatic door just ahead of a potbellied man in an elegantly pale golf shirt—stepping on his loafer—the taxi's automated back door already opening—

He knows where to go—

Okay, yes, she says—*I understand*—

Is she back in character?—she resists again—

But I don't—why is it that S wants to be her—or to be his mother's lover?

It's not a matter of want, her husband says—*You'll see—he can't help it—he's that—*

Her—

Yes—her—and much more—I'm not sure we can know how much—

But you, she says—begins to say—in Japanese—

The long time has started—the dose she'd consumed—shortly before they landed—finally beginning to take effect—engulfing her—just as Serizawa said it would—

Her husband hasn't heard—continues to talk—as if in another language—

And she likes the sound—just a sound—like the far-off shrill of an insect—the roar of ever rising waves—*a feeling of release from my real face*—

The white-gloved driver—filled with the most intense feelings of sorrow and regret—merges into traffic—enchanted by that face in the mirror—its manly curve—a face he could not have tired of looking at—

But he knows where to go—knows he must deliver her to Room 2082—

Those last permissible pleasures they shared in private—

You wander aimlessly for some time—a bit like a man who's been in an accident—far from home—up there in the halls above the pandemonium of the market floor—swimming ashore against dense black waves of workers—office ladies and executives—stevedores and auctioneers—a courier riding a bicycle—ringing his bell again and again—somehow navigating through the crowd without ever having to touch one foot to the ground—

With S gone—there would be no chance—no way to be sure what Serizawa is really up to—or was—because it's possible now that the long time has finally started and—no matter what you do—you're too late—the great wave is already on the threshold—and hundreds of thousands will be receiving the same nasty dose tonight—

Entering what seems like an empty office—just for a moment—to escape the crowd—you sit at the Noguchi coffee table—

Are you sure it was her—inside the tuna?

You make the call but there's no answer—

There's a sound behind the desk and then a woman emerges from behind a folding screen—short and wide—fortyish—lumbering—almost limping—

Why is she looking at you that way?—as if she recognizes you—despite the surgical mask—the wig and dark glasses—

Ah, she says—*you're early*—

And how did she know to speak English?

Come, she says, *come back*—beckoning you so urgently you can't resist—as if—as if that hand engenders a dark current—pulling you out to sea—

Through a short passage—past shelves filled with what appear to be patient files—the phone on the desk behind you starting to ring—ringing and ringing—

Into the examination room—where a body lies facedown beneath a clean sheet—only its buttocks exposed—so white and beautiful—male or female—you're not sure—the legs slightly spread—prepared for whatever procedure is about to take place—

The doctor—face concealed by his mask—nevertheless seems familiar—his eyes—the dramatic crease between them—almost as if you may be looking into a mirror—but you're distracted by the presence—the weedy smell—of the kappa beside him—also gowned and masked—prepared to walk him through it all—the two of them wearing gloves edged with black fur—

This way—the woman says—that hand drawing you on—guiding you through an open shōji into the adjoining room—a Japanese room—the two physicians left muttering behind you—an awful noise back there—and then the secret door behind the tokonoma sliding open to reveal a gravel path—leading beneath a torii—into a dense bamboo grove—

Go on—the woman says—that hand on your back now—pressing you forward—and you go—certain that this may actually be your very last chance to stop him—the very last chance to end it—

He got caught up in a variety of fantasies—
which could have settled his soul—

I would like to construct a huge countryside in Tokyo–

There were other reasons—

She'd discovered some irregularities, she said—reviewing the paperwork submitted by one of the auction houses—the one where M works—though she still doesn't know about this—still thinks he's in telecom—

Anyway they've been investing heavily in something recorded in their ledgers only as Y—

Is it some kind of equipment? Some property somewhere? A new kind of fishing vessel?

Her boss—K-san—had seemed surprised by the pattern—said he'd look into it—but a week later—at their scheduled meeting—he'd forgotten—or claimed to—until she provided further details—then he said he'd interviewed some people himself—(in fact, he'd warned M not to be so careless—he was leaving tracks—but that's what cute little cats do—because M was still young and beautiful and he couldn't ease up)—it was nothing, K-san said—an irregularity—an internal matter that had gotten someone fired—that's all—might as well forget it and move on—

But the pattern emerged again soon after—not quite as pronounced—just a faint signature of—what?—manipulation?—perversion?—a crime?—but who was—or would be—the victim?—she wasn't sure—but she felt certain—certain there would be a victim—victims—the market—or maybe the capital—or maybe worse—

To ignore it would lead to catastrophe—

She felt as certain about this—she told K-san—as one does when experiencing the onset of a grave illness—

You're a hypochondriac, K-san laughed—when she explained it like that—walking him through the faint evidence—and again he insisted there was nothing there—that he'd known the men she was accusing since they were at school together—that he had no reason to ever suspect them of wrongdoing—and that if she persisted in suggesting otherwise—he would be inclined to reprimand her—which would likely disqualify her from the live-birth trial in which she was participating—

Ah, K-san laughed again—*you thought I didn't know—*

She lowered her head—ashamed of her ambition—though she didn't want to be—not anymore—and yet there it was—a kind of collar—or just a rope—as if she'd been born with it around her neck—around her wrists and ankles—constricting everything—kinbaku style—

I've told no one about it, she said—*just as Tomotoki instructed us—*

That impulse makes you so valuable, S-san—

He'd been a good mentor to her before—before this—very kind—because she had no family, she supposed—an orphan—her parents taken by disease—The Disease—in its early years—before its source was known—the disease they all carried now—on the inside—like the tuna's hidden burn—their bodies—her body—toxic to sperm and egg—the condition tracked back to some defective, hybrid bluefin distributed during the Heisei era—

And—probably—he was kind, too, because his only son—Y—a beautiful hard-partying danshi—was a disappointment—or that's how he put it—

And anyway, she said—*I didn't want to have to explain to anyone—in case I couldn't—in case my body couldn't—improve—*

But I'm the one who recommended you, K-san said—*didn't you suspect?—I happen to be very good friends with Dr. Tomotoki—please remember that—and that he'll keep me apprised of your progress—so that I can replace you quickly—when you become pregnant—*

Her parents' withering—skin turning pale—spongy—then flaking into white powder—covering them completely—hairless—almost gender-less—that sour smell—undiagnosed—undiagnosable—in those early days—after their migration to America—where she was born—something else no one knew—seemed to know—not even Yumiko—not even M—who she'd found she couldn't resist—(such a mysterious flavor!)—who'd become more to her than just a fellow participant at the lab—their mouths seeming to become one as they sucked each other's tongues—

Later—at lunch—she decided to tell Yumiko everything—just in case—about the experiment—about M—his beauty and kindness—his scent—the feel of him in her hand—

Her suspicions—

Why—she wondered—did her friend seem so subdued as she talked—so indifferent—not even asking for more explicit details about the sex—Yumiko's usual topic?

It actually made S angry—didn't Yumiko understand that she was risking her life on this project?—or anyway that's how it seemed—

Because what if Tomotoki and his crew discovered that she wasn't really Japanese?

The display of knives around the lab couldn't mean nothing—

Don't you trust K-san? Yumiko asked—*he's always treated you well*—

As if she really knew something about it—

And though her friend had been looking down at the platter of sushi between them—apparently undecided between the salmon and the sea urchin—(neither farmed in Dàlián as everyone supposed—but made

from Yamato—which has already infiltrated the market—untested—
and is paying off tremendously!)—S thought later—on her way to meet
M at the love hotel behind Hanayashiki—that it felt as if Yumiko had
been staring right at her—staring through her even—her gaze like an
air pistol—aimed right at her speckled nose—carefully powdered as always—to conceal the truth—

Yumiko seemed to be regarding her—in fact—with the same look S had
received once from a man on the Hibiya Line—who—in the morning
crush—had slipped a hand between her legs—as if evaluating her for
quality—ignoring her face—which he must have felt was incapable of
displaying anything substantial about what he might find inside—

And how afraid she'd been—even then—feeling her foreignness burning
beneath the powder—her hidden, inner foreignness warm against his
probing fingers—afraid that he might turn to the man next to him and
complain *oh, but she's not Japanese*—

I was a child then and hadn't yet had
any near-death experience—

I'm sure they'll be walking in the door any minute–

Three small children were wandering at the edge of the pond in Sudo Park—throwing stones—hurling them as if at a moving target—at the red and white-gold koi maybe—

M watching them from a bench up the slope—wondering about their common cruelty and waiting for his contact—listening to the rush of the park's tall cascade—one hand on the hinoki box—

Inside—the sashimi knife that he'd purchased from Katagiri—cherry blossoms engraved on its blade—

In the darkness—beneath the maples—the kids are little more than shapes—forms made of shadow—edged with black fur—

They could be dogs or foxes—feral—neighbors—one drags a red carp banner behind him—found—or stolen from a shrine—blown from its mooring by the previous night's storm—caught on the eaves—

The kids get up on the red-railed bridge to the Benten-dō—taking aim at the fish once more before crossing all the way—two wandering around the back of the shrine—the other stepping down to the water—

The action there is quick—as the kid wades in—shoes still on—a little wave rushing forward—seeming to become an arm—and he's gone—the red koinobori left behind—all flat on the gravel—

The other two reemerge—saunter down to the water's edge like the oth-er—call out to him—the pond like a cave's mouth—its reflective surface an illusion—the kids standing on the cusp of a deep hole to the inside—

Then the wave—the arm—and the carp again alone—

His own arm—half raised as if to take a stroke—to move him forward through dark breakers—toward a still-distant shore—or further out to sea—M watches his hand descend again to its place on his own thigh—

A young couple emerges from the sushiya across the street—you can sense it working on them—you can smell it—

A small light—a bubble coming up—

The sound of a bicycle passing—creak of chain—rusting wheel—springs—

Of clouds passing close—

Of a frog leaping from the water—leaping up—but not landing—not yet—

A luminous thing hanging there—like an ancient mirror—risen gently into the air above the water's dark surface—a heart-sized object of indistinct shape—his desire—

Fleshlike—an organ—a substance—a thing from the interior—

As if he'd expelled it there—the very eye from his head—

A drop of silent liquid—

Shirikodama, Y called it?

Curved and supple—the ache—illumination—sperm and egg—roe—a thing that allows—that drives—that opens and accepts—cleaves and becomes—obscene in the extraction—that stinks of guts—intensifying every pleasure—as it goes down—

And his shape there—inside—M—where he feels its pulsing—its whirl-pool heart—

A gob of spit—

Get used to me in you, she wrote—

The shape of her—too—her Japanese face—that mask of the woman—lit by moonlight—and white powder—oshiroi—S—standing there
in the grove—melting on your tongue—that sound above—of the tall
green stalks of bamboo—knocking together in the wind—the same as
the hyōshige—as the Kabuki's curtain flies open—

Washed ashore—far from home—

And the sensation of entering—through the mirrored hall—as if for the
first time—through the mouth—the body of the beautiful Japanese—
himself—ingested—made flesh—

A kind of mikoshi—this floating thing—the god's palanquin—transport-
ing itself—like a fish—the swift tuna—a lateral shuddering against the
wall of air—flying toward the lower entrance—and M—ecstatic—rising
too—and following after—ever closer to her—

Men really have strange emotions when resolving upon death–

As the black-clad runner opens the curtain to the accompaniment of the hyōshige—the girl—wearing a warrior's costume and aragoto make-up—thick black wig trailing down her back—tightens the final knot that pulls M—on his back—into position—head drawn up from the floor toward his bound knees and feet—his nude body powdered entirely white—

She rolls him over with her straw-sandaled foot—from his back onto his legs—forced by the bindings into a splayed lotus position—the whole network of cords and loops constricting him in an uncomfortable arc—facing the audience—head suspended over his feet—bound arms crooked above and behind his head—wrists fastened at midback—

A structure—yes—Yoritomo seems to satisfy himself—nodding as he circles the captive—the bound body a kind of mikoshi—a little mirrored hall—edged with black fur—

And what god might answer when she knocks?

The chorus of shamisen plucking through a steady melody—the plover flute winging circles overhead—while the interrogator brushes her riding crop across his back—locates a rib and presses down—increasing the pressure until M withdraws sharply—

Tell us—Mrs.—why you've returned—why you're seeking the whereabouts of your so-called child—abandoned in the shallows—so long ago—

The script is improvised—both actors' choices unknown to the other before the performance—what M chooses to reveal or conceal is up to him—and the girl's part has its own parameters—a predetermined range of questions and actions—a time limit—necessary given the discomfort of the shrimp-tie—a general ceiling for the amount of pain to be administered—

Whether or not there will be blood—

Wasn't there an agreement—Mrs.?

It was him that contacted me, M says—*seeking—I don't know—a new connection—*

The girl swings her arm through an easy arc—as if returning a tennis ball—the sound of the strike—every strike—obscured—by the clap of the hyōshige offstage—the sound of theater—

Except that M's grimace suggests authentic pain—

Then again—there is no pain—only motion and sound—

The girl holds her position on the follow through—crossing her eyes—snapping her head toward the audience to make the soft, bristled wig ripple—shouts of her stage name come out of the balcony—

You signed a contract, she purrs—

But I can't stop him from reaching out—the woodblock sounding as the riding crop touches his right ear—a drop of blood falling on his calf—*I won't— if he needs me—wants me back—his mother—*

That bridge is crossed—

We will never reach the other side—

The girl rakes the crop slowly over his ribs—a sort of caress—pausing at his nipple—the visible form of invisibility—the illusion of a breast—and she gazes back out into the audience where she said she would be seated—the real one—M's wife—by the hanamichi—

But she's not there!

She won't talk will she?

Because—too—he wanted to warn me—

Eh—

Had already explained about Y, M says—reverting to a young girl's tones and head movements—activating all those behaviors' traditional associations with purity—naïveté—despite everything—his gaijin eyes—their shape and color—the man everyone knows is inside the body—behind the powder—

Codename: Yamato, she trills—

The girl's manly laugh turns to a growl—but M can't ease up—

—*and the operation at Dàlián*, M goes on—almost a question—*the stockpiling—the secret distribution of that substance—the substitute*—

The girl lashes M twice—

S wanting to withdraw himself from the trial—and Serizawa—what the hell is he really up to?

Blood dripping from his right ear—he hadn't—maybe—meant to use the real name—not exactly—but now—

The interrogator's foot wedged up under his ass—wriggling her toes against his balls—not painful yet—but uncomfortable—the chafing of the straw sandal—a move they've never rehearsed—or even discussed—

She could silence him whenever she wants this way—control him with the flexing of her toes—grab—pinch—pull—

So—it was a setup!

Still he can sense the audience beginning to shift toward him—feeling his unease—not quite as predatory—not quite as eager as they were—for the failure of his performance—

(Wasn't that desire expected—the reason given for the lackluster ticket sales—and then also for the great demand—at the last minute—for the most expensive seats—where Kabuki's real aficionados—those most invested in its protection—its preservation—and in the gaijin's debacle—could sit in pleasurable judgment of his arrogance?)

(Not so much an appropriation—he's argued of his performance—as an intervention in authenticity—a slowly won self-awareness—an intentional failure to express the pleasures and perfidy of Western longing through its glowing—dream-like—fictional Easts—the enactment of those *impenetrable Japans* hypothesized by Melville—those hard-on pre-Meiji Western sailors on the threshold—locked out of the double-bolted shogunate—threatened with imprisonment and torture should they come ashore—intoxicated by scents of cherry and cedar drifting across the offing—by the willowy white bodies awaiting them amongst the bamboo and pines—)

(Even now that they've long since been taken into the mouth—those imagined Japanese bodies remain the source—M has said—of all his wanting—)

(I must be—he has told me—a miserable bricolage of error—)

(Meaning by this not an apology by way of self-recognition—seeing his woman emerge unsteadily from the mirror—followed immediately by another—gloves edged with black fur—)

(—but rather his internal imperative—that he must be—he must—)

Blood dripping—almost streaming from his ear—

Growing anxious now—the sparse audience—the iki, feline epicures in deep shadow—anxious about their own failure—because their bellies are full of it again tonight—the monster—as they've known from the start—

(No reason to deny it anymore—M—the gaijin—their mirror—)

Y—already turning circles in their guts—turning them on—urging them—dragging them—no matter their age—toward a catastrophic spawning—a great millenarianasm—a release of that dark wave of material—higher than Mount Sumeru—

The great blooming of every mizuko ever—

Like petals raining down—engulfing the capital and sucking it out to sea—making way—as has been planned—for the Japan of Tomorrow—

She's straddled M from behind—squatting on his back—pressing down with all her weight—to shut him down—close him up—more clam than shrimp—the muscles in his lower back—hips—thighs—shoulders—burning—though he remains flexible as—supple as—womanly possible—

Yamato is poison, he squeezes out—words almost lost against the wildly palpitating hyōshige—the hand drums and shamisen—the chorus of voices too—approaching a noisy crescendo—reminding me of the convulsions of intercourse—

A genomic translator—rewriting everything—everyone—into a nearly pure unity—a devastating monoculture—except for one flaw—that lying clean-shaven face—

She's pulsing herself against the knot fastening his wrists—using it for stimulus as she whips him without mercy—left—right—arms—legs—head—like a fading horse—driving him into darkness—

But he no longer feels it—nor hears—only the reverberations of the hyōshige—and her body against his—the thrum of her shouts—fury and pleasure—sweat—blood—come running down his back—the beating of his heart—hers—the two of them finishing together—collapsing into the sound of the curtain-runner's feet—

Then applause—

Then the siren—

The sound of a bell resounds
through the twilight–

The late program at the Kabuki-za has just ended when I arrive at the mirrored office tower—sprung like a knife from the back of the white-faced theater—

The exiting crowd is phenomenal—exquisitely Japanese—older women in their modest kimonos—appropriately hued for their age and the season—deep plum—eel brown—

The older men—several wearing jaunty straw boaters—emphasizing the nostalgia of the costume—insisting on a Taishō mise-en-scène—

And all their younger, modern companions in black—the visible form of invisibility to the gaijin eye—like the puppeteers of Bunraku—ignored by the audience in favor of these mellow bursts of drama—color—tasteful lines—

Upstairs—everyone working late, of course—the company's offices—a sea of cubicles really—somber and plain—a bland incubator for their large and varied portfolio of theater and film productions—weirdly quiet—the individual spaces—lit by the workers' desk lamps and glowing screens—

The secretary actually draws me a map to my destination—on a tiny pad seemingly made for this purpose—

How could I have known then that it would be you?

Or why had I never suspected?

Turning the corner—I've come face-to-face—as if striking a mirror—my face on yours—as if it's been stolen—like a mask—except—Japanese—Japanned, as Barthes says—cited and transformed—

Not inherited—as if you were some long-lost child—

But the very face—

And all you can say is *Oh—it's you—such excellent timing—these production mock-ups have just arrived—*

Which is what finally drops me—because there I am—you—we—again—again—and again—as if we really had entered some mirrored hall—

Walk!—the girl shouts—in one hand a sashimi knife—blade etched with cherry blossoms—in the other a syringe—the man's shirt already off—a long, bleeding cut on his arm—

Late one night, he says in voice-over—*she showed up to our Western-style house—right in the middle of everything—indifferent to one who has suffered misfortune—*

Isn't that the detective from that other show? M wonders—

Five steps and he's at the top of the stairs—the floor seeming to suck at the soles of his shoes—but apparently he can't ease up—

In two or three steps, he says—*the sake brought a tipsy feeling of release—*

She instructs him to leave his shoes by the door—the Japanese way—toes pointing down the hall—already anticipating his exit—

Don't worry, he says—lowering his head—licking his master's hand—*I'll do it—what you want—*

Don't worry, she says, *you're going to sleep!*—jabbing the syringe into his arm—depressing the plunger as if detonating a bomb—forcing the clear liquid in—

Close up: his gaping mouth—edged by a thin, sweaty moustache—terror and ecstasy—

Come doggy, she commands—brushing past him—advancing like the Tokugawa shogun toward the ludicrous bed—shaped like a scallop shell—a baroquely carved frame of gleaming dark wood—the upper half of the shell—the headboard—standing open against the wall—upholstered with pearl-colored silk—the same as the sheets—

She lets her skirt slip off—the detective following behind—

She removes her camisole—revealing seven black stripes—curving around the right side of her body—one reaching to her lower back—ending in a small spiral above the cleft of her plum-shaped ass—

Beside the bed—she makes a slow turn—lies back—a waterbed, of course—the stripes widening across her torso—an octopus's legs—the eighth leg encircling her right breast—the thing's head—her left breast—nipple inked black as well—a visible protrusion just below the glaring eye—

Would she taste of it, M wonders—*that darkness?*

She raises her feet to his hips—grabs his ass with the toes of her left foot—slides the right up his chest—hooking it around his neck—pulling him in close—closer to her shadow—

How long does he have, M wonders—*before whatever dose she's injected begins to take effect?*

The undulating bed—the light—her breathing—make the octopus swim—

He reaches for her extended leg—that supple, edible thigh—but too slow—she's slashed his hand!—blood spurting onto her stomach—

Oh Yoko!—she's not sure why she agreed to let them use her real name—

And now she's got his cock at knifepoint—and *why*, she wonders, *do I still feel a little scared?*

She was able to earn a bit extra to pay for the procedure by spitting in a few wealthy fans' faces after shows—but M and S started giving her a hard time about it—that that was Sumotori Honeymoon's thing—her thing as the band's front man, sure—but she was representing all three of them—the band's attitude—its rebellious aggression—its brutal sexuality—so she shouldn't commodify it like that—shouldn't recontextualize it—repackage it—offer it for sale—like some fucking T-shirt—

So she had to find another way—and quick before they figured out she was pregnant—

Using the foot on his shoulder she forces the weakened detective to his knees—thrusts herself into his face—as she's been instructed—

Oh—oh—Yoko—lapping at her like a German Shepherd—

Y's offer of a part in this pink film seemed straight enough—but it's the way they all look at her—those guys just off camera—chinpira she recognizes from around Tsukiji—from when they were kids together—what do they call themselves now?—The Pure Land Group?—the octopus they've painted on her—the gang's kamon—(at first, they'd insisted on a real tattoo)—like she's theirs now—which she'll never be—and this feels too close to home maybe—but whatever—after tonight she'll be done—she'll get the abortion and next stop—Sumotori Honeymoon headlining in Hollywood—

Until—out of nowhere—a sword slices the guy's head off—his neck fountaining—how the blade didn't take off her leg as well M has no idea—but that's movies—a weird edit then—as she's screaming so authentically—to a point-of-view shot of a beautiful young Japanese standing there—framed by her bare, bloody thighs—a salaryman in a black suit—the belly of his gleaming white shirt speckled with the other man's blood—

I knew I couldn't trust you, he says—raising the sword—a maguro bōchō—over his head—*this is a lifetime deal*—

But Yoko's too quick—*Tokyo stinks,* she says—(an ad lib)—gutting him with the sashimi knife—

Then a screech of tires outside and the shooting starts—the chinpira breaking for the exits—one of them going down in the doorway—dragged off by the others—and then *fuck*, she's thinking—*now I'm not getting paid*—

M-san, she calls out as she shuts off the shower—

What do you need?—he should probably change the channel—he wouldn't want her to know he's so crass—just another beastly American salivating over—

Nothing—I was just—

I'm exhausted—but he's still watching as the girl looks out the window—at a man downstairs—on the corner—wearing a surgical mask—a wig and dark glasses—

I was thinking, she says from the doorway—wrapping a towel around her hair—*that we work very well together—that we make an excellent team—onstage—don't you agree?*

Her face a shadow—

Seeing himself in there—in that dark mirror—in which she is Yoritomo—

Looking at M on the bed—M recumbent—the pose so natural—as if he'd been holding it his whole life—his still-damp body—the towel around his waist—the bulge of his erect cock—body lit by the action on the screen—black-suited yakuza sword fighting like samurai in a Western bedroom—

M—my odalisque, she's thinking—*my Oriental—my object—my—my—*

In her hand—the sashimi knife—blade etched with cherry blossoms—waiting for his answer—

Once or twice–every single day–
dressed as the goddess Izanami–

I come to on a cot—in a dim room—barely more than a closet—smelling of rubbing alcohol and latex—S sitting in a chair beside my head—her face—her—

Yes—

Her—

Isn't that right?

Something about the light before—in the cubicle—the half light—deceptive—or the late hour—all the stress of the day's shoot—exhaustion—that made him seem like—more—S—a beautiful young Japanese—but what is it?—that manly curve—my own face—and hers—hers—a mirror, too—that white cheek emitting its own low glow—the whiteness of the Japanese—those parted lips—

Take this, she'd offered—after laying me down—covering me with a blanket—chin-length hair draping her cheek—

A black tablet—*don't chew—just grind slowly between your back teeth*—

As if whispering—*oh—I love you—I want*—

Your tongue like an inkstone—

Fish—pine—clove—such a mysterious flavor—

You didn't have to stay, I'm saying—

Oh I've just come back, M-san—just sat down here—I must have wakened you—how do you feel?

What I feel is a strange energy radiating from my gut—turned on—a hard-on—a tingling around the lips and rectum—

Like we should get back to work, I guess—sitting up—

Ah, she sighs—*time for that—all night*—her hand on my shoulder—ambiguous and fine—a floral scent I can't quite place—*let's walk first*—

The rooftop garden—she says—was constructed as a miniature version of Bashō's journey to the Deep North—a model of the poet's riverside hut—beneath a bonsai banana tree—on our right as we exit the building onto the gravel path—following it counterclockwise—along the little stream toward Senju—lit stone lanterns set among the stones and ponds—on the hills of dwarf pines—creating a serene and romantic atmosphere—cut loose from the city—rising gently into the air—like a warm fragrance—cedar incense—the midnight traffic of Ginza far below—

I'm sorry for your trouble, M-san—

No, I say—*no trouble—I was—this production—the Tsukiji project*—remembering now that it was my doing—that I was the one who set up the appointment—that I'm the one—that I—that I meant to be the one—the one in the mock-ups—that I cast myself as the husband—hers—the first one—the Japanese—and why should I forget?—

That is—we've just started—but—I've hardly had time to sleep since I arrived—so maybe I need to rest is all—

A whiff of sulfur marks the Murder Stone north of Kurobane—close by, a willow—then the unohana—blooming clouds of white flowers beside the barrier-gate of Shirakawa—the grass—stones—pathway covered with petals—

No, S says—*it's not you—it's your wife*—

Gloves edged with black fur—working up into—

His wife, I say—

All right—

Still—and always, I think—continuing on—the first one—the Japanese—
and she's back at his house tonight—at their house—in Bunkyo ward—
probably showering after the flight—a surprise—for him—though he's
still at his office—no doubt—will be—for a few more hours—until Tsukiji closes—about the time I'll need to be back on set—to play him—isn't
that it?—and what if we should meet?

And I'll be yours—her lips parted invitingly—

To replace her—my wife—to substitute—like masks—each for the other—her and him and me and she—with a real Japanese—the plot of
our film—this one—playing out exactly the same in real life—

Her hand in mine—S—due to bear our child—once the long time has
finally started—

Our mouths seem to become one as we suck each other's tongues—

You still taste like her, she says—

But I haven't—we haven't—but how could she know how she tastes?—my
wife?—why should she remember a thing like that?

It's all right—she wipes her mouth—blood on her thumb—*I mean like a
gaijin—an acquired taste*—her smile so handsome I feel rather inadequate—

Sure—

But don't pout—you're not ashamed—

This is not a question—and I want to be careful—because this one can
be cruel—a knife slitting open the belly—

Hell no, I say—stepping to the edge of the Shadow Pond—an empty
mirror—looking back to find dark clouds occluding the moon—

It's just that—the time—I think—the desire she—Yoko—my wife—and I have shared all these years for some—thing—else—before meeting and after—a kind of ambition maybe—but—how shallow!

She's settled herself on a stone—showing me her profile—*But who cares?*

Isn't it something like buying a car—or choosing a cat?

I hate cats—

Settling for the poor translation—for each other in the meantime—the Japanese face—

Oh—but she's not Japanese—

Yes—just a mask—I know—but—

And I'm irritated and we drift on—like those sluggish clouds—

Only the suggestion of real pleasure—Yoko and me—an obscure dream of green silk—a souvenir of Tokyo—a warm scent—the far-off sound of a koto—*like a bat that passes for a bird*, she said—just as ambivalent with me as she'd become with the first one—the real Japanese—except—staying apart from him had only stoked the craving—(for me in this picture)— mine and hers—for him—for his authenticity—our perverse sense of— taking him in hand—into the mouth—them—one—some Japanese—S—

Come, she says—holding out her hand again—drawing me close—

Choosing him—choosing that—because it was possible for us—people like us—our decadence—our desire—our American violence—

Don't worry, she says—lowering her head—*I'll do it—what you want—*

Just like that—like this—she'd offered herself—reaching out to her old friend at just the right time it seemed—just to say *ohayō*—she said—to

Yoko—to us—S—something quite exquisite—we agreed—S—melting on your tongue—

It's here, she says—*where Aika landed*—*near the islands of Matsushima*—the two of us looking up—toward the nineteenth-floor balcony—as if she were still on the way down—eyes closed—black hair spreading around her—opening like wings—

Someone up there—on the balcony—looking down—watching us I think—a man?—maybe her boss—K-san—or—

And I would have, too—*thrown myself over*—*if*—

No, I say—*no*—our lips almost touching—

Someone's watching us—

I know—

Izanami and Izanagi—that's the two of us—to die to that other life—to choose death and start again—somewhere in the western suburbs—never to be them—I know—to be born Japanese—I can never—but to have S—to be so very close—at last—

Come, she says—and *Yes,* I say—as she leads me into the grove—

How have we—or really they—the Japanese—developed such appetites, she won-ders, *such bad taste—such vulgarity?*

The disaster film's images of dark waves flooding Tokyo are reminiscent of—if not based on—all the most traumatic footage from Tōhoku—and maybe also on some survivors' detailed memories of that day—though the action here takes place on a moonlit night—no doubt to catch more people in the midst of joy—rather than the drudgery of work—

But so many—like him—are still working!

Office towers and apartment buildings come down—Skytree—Tokyo Tower—the Mori building—the Kabuki-za—the merchant stalls of Asakusa—there goes the National Diet building—and the Supreme Court—

But why, she wonders—*don't they show the destruction of the Imperial Palace or Yasukuni?*

There is some subtext in this—she suspects—a deeply conservative de-sire for renewal—a reassertion of essential values following a test of national character—isn't that always the case with these films?

A fascistic ethos taking pleasure in the winnowing of society to a few individuals—representative types—whose subsequent psychological and physical struggles leave—finally—just two categories—the weak and the strong—and one beautiful, white-skinned woman—a jewel of perfect health and strength—to bear the new generation as the sun rises again—

And yet—it's hard to understand how anyone might survive this sce-nario—

She's just come out of the shower—so she has no idea if the film is be-ginning or if it's nearing the end—no idea if the disaster was man-made or natural—though that hardly matters at this point beyond thematics—

In any case—things don't look good for humans—and they're getting worse—

Is this Osaka now?—Hiroshima?—Fukuoka?—the whole archipelago's gone under, it seems—bullet trains—fishing boats—tiny cars and trucks—is that ASIMO?—a drowned sumo wrestler floats by—a couple of samurai and a geisha—men and women in kimonos—their faces painted for the Kabuki—cut to: a lidless tea caddy decorated with an exquisitely stylized black pine in gold—a maid café girl—a koto—a hand drum—some straw sandals—one tall geta—and an open red parasol—a blue-faced salaryman—a pink-haired Lolita trailing black lace—

Every representation—every cliché—of Japaneseness beloved by the West—by her, too—has died—

So now—she sits on the edge of her bed—their bed once—before their troubles—before their own catastrophe—the very heart of their tastefully appointed Western-style bedroom—

She wraps a second towel around her wet hair—starting to feel—in spite of her impulsive critique of this spectacle—some anticipation—what might take that other Japan's place?

The camera pans right and travels through the open bedroom door— the sounds of rising water on the television behind us still the only soundtrack—fading as we cross a darkened passageway into the Japanese room—the slow, smooth approach to the tokonoma gives us time to read the characters that her husband wrote—some time ago—after she left—on the hanging scroll behind the white peonies arranged in an ancient vase—

Who would be happy to go to his death?—reads the subtitle—

As close as we can get—before we dissolve through the back of the tokonoma—to a narrow landing at the top of a staircase descending into darkness—all the way to Dàlián—to the most impure world of illusion—

Gentle footsteps—almost like dripping water—and then a slim figure emerging from below—wearing the uniform of a Tokyo Imperial University student—

Five steps to the top of the stairs—the sashimi knife in one hand—blade etched with cherry blossoms—his powdered neck visible above the high collar—face half in shadow—red-lacquered lips—a long lock of hair lying against one cheek making her identity even more uncertain—

A fine performer of Japanese ancestry—whispers the voice-over—

Gloves edged with black fur slide open the secret door—

Then a screech of tires—then the shooting starts—

Her face appears in the bedroom window—beside the silk curtain—

Does she see him?—M—standing there on the corner—motioning for her to come down—to come over the balcony—come quickly—before it's too late?

It's too late—she's disappeared—and the detective is coming out of the grove at the end of the street—half dragging his leg—the product of a misunderstanding—the air pistol in his hand—M dodging behind a planter—

Back to work!

Then the shooting starts—

It's too late—

The long time has finally started, M-san!

The woman is not defenseless—but now all the lights in the house are out—

She showed up right in the middle of everything—indifferent to misfortune—

New methods for new times!

When the artillery fire finally stops—M draws his hand back—(a sashimi knife?—a mirror?)—and rises gently into the air—to take the other man out—

Just what the hell is Serizawa working on?

It's impossible, though—

There will be no reply—

Lying there—between the taxi—the crow—the baby carriage—the man
only looks on and harmonizes—

His legs gone—

His gills—

He'll keep it a secret—

And then the siren sounds—this film's background music—

And a radiant moon comes out—

And the capital is engulfed by a sudden wave—

He will not use my name—or his—
There is no need—

At dawn on the morning of the fifth day of the fifth month—her slim hands slide open the cardboard shelter as if it were a shōji—the girl—Yoko—in a pearl-colored shift—standing—extending her arms to the sky—arching her back in an extravagant stretch that forces the last warm breath of sleep from her—

An elderly homeless man—(once an executive at a major bank)—is already awake—seated on a folding stool—a few meters further down the walkway between the park and Ueno station—heating water over a gas camp stove—reading yesterday's *Asahi* with great dignity—

The headline on the front page declares: *Yamato Is Poison!*

Otsukare sama desu, the girl says—but the man does not respond—

The southbound train departs—full of them all—

She bends down and retrieves the sashimi knife—blade etched with cherry blossoms—from the slit belly of the massive bluefin tuna—the biggest we've ever seen—then begins shuffling toward the park—back toward Tsukiji—trailing a long strand of kombu behind her—stuck to her foot like it's been a long night—like she's come a very long way—

I am huge, she mutters—as the old man and the station vanish—

The park, too—the concert hall—the Museum of Western Art—the National Museum—the zoo—

Spreading erasure like a stain—a spilled, silent liquid—Asakusa—Yanaka—Arakawa Ward—gone—

Only whiteness left in her wake—whiteness rolling on ahead of her, too—a great wave—

A blank sheet of mulberry paper—

An uninterpretable chrysanthemum silence—

NOTES ON SOURCES

Quoted material appears on the following pages:

12 "[In] the old days, even the most inconsequential people were impressive": Sei Shōnagon, *The Pillow Book*, translated by Meredith McKinney, New York: Penguin Classics, 2007.

61 "written very beautifully on thin blue paper": Sei Shōnagon, *The Pillow Book*, translated by Meredith McKinney, New York: Penguin Classics, 2007.

70 "In a certain reign [...] someone of no very great rank, among all His Majesty's Consorts and Intimates, enjoyed exceptional favor": Murasaki Shikibu, *The Tale of Genji*, translated by Royall Tyler, New York: Penguin Books, 2003.

80 and 82 "You shouldn't mess with me / I'll ruin everything you are": David Bowie and Iggy Pop, "China Girl," *The Idiot*, RCA Records, 1977.

94 "It will sometimes burst from out that cloudless sky, like an exploding bomb upon a dazed and sleepy town": Herman Melville, *Moby-Dick*, New York: W.W. Norton, 2002.

111 "In fact every month according to its season the year round is delightful": Sei Shōnagon, *The Pillow Book*, translated by Meredith McKinney, New York: Penguin Classics, 2007.

113 "And why do I paint my lips and blacken my teeth? / It is because I love you, because / I am happy": "Musume Dojoji," *Six Kabuki Plays*, translated by Donald Richie and Miyoko Watanabe, Tokyo: Hokuseido Press, 1963.

115 "Do you know how a man feels when he is bound by long black hair": Natsume Sōseki, *Kokoro*, translated by Ineko Sato, Tokyo: Hokuseido Press, 1941.

139 "Born of the illicit union between dream and reality": Yukio Mishima, "Onnagata," *Death in Midsummer and Other Stories*, translated by Geoffrey Sargent, New York: New Directions, 1966.

166 "Your gestures must be more gentle . . . . You need to appear more than just tender and gentle . . . . You must switch off your own body . . . . you must portray her inner feelings": Nakamura Shibajaku, *Portrait of an Onnagata: The Female Impersonator in Kabuki*, Films for the Humanities & Sciences, 1990.

180 "One does not need to be dazzling like an alien from another star": Tatsumi Hijikata, "Man, Once Dead, Crawl Back!" *The Twentieth Century Performance Reader*, Abingdon (UK): Routledge, 2013.

185 "Do whatever it is you people do": David Bowie, quoting Nagisa Ōshima (slightly modified), "Bowie at the Bijou," *David Bowie: The Last Interview and Other Conversations*, New York: Melville House Publishing, 2016.

188 "Like a bat that passes for a bird": Matsuo Bashō, "A Visit to Kashima Shrine," *The Narrow Road to the Deep North and Other Travel Sketches*, translated by Nobuyuki Yuasa, New York: Penguin Classics, 1967.

202 "There are various ways of escaping from the world of illusion, but in these unclean tumultuous latter days of the Law, the best one is to recite the name of the Amida Buddha": *Tale of the Heike*, translated by Helen Craig McCullough, Stanford: Stanford UP, 1988.

221 "as a thousand leagues of blue . . . that serene ocean rolling eastwards . . . sweet mystery and awful stirrings . . . already on the

threshold": Herman Melville, *Moby-Dick*, New York: W.W. Norton, 2002.

236 "I would like to construct a huge countryside in Tokyo": Tatsumi Hijikata, "Man, Once Dead, Crawl Back!" *The Twentieth Century Performance Reader*, Abingdon (UK): Routledge, 2013.

253 "The sound of a bell resounds through the twilight": "Musume Dojoji," *Six Kabuki Plays*, translated by Donald Richie and Miyoko Watanabe, Tokyo: Hokuseido Press, 1963.

The images on pages 129, 144, 193, 256, 257, and 258 were created by YAMAGUCHI Akira; © YAMAGUCHI Akira, courtesy of Mizuma Art Gallery.

Additionally, Parts II and III of *TOKYO* include a number of mashups, sentences and phrases drawing from multiple texts. That material was appropriated from the following sources:

Abe, Kobo. *The Face of Another*. Translated by E. Dale Saunders. New York: Perigee, 1966.

———. *Inter Ice Age 4*. Translated by E. Dale Saunders. New York: Perigee, 1981.

Akutagawa, Ryonusuke. "In a Grove." *Rashomon and Other Stories*. Translated by Takashi Kojima. New York: Bantam Books, 1952.

———. "Rashomon." *Rashomon and Other Stories*. Translated by Takashi Kojima. New York: Bantam Books, 1952.

Barthes, Roland. *Empire of Signs*. Translated by Richard Howard. New York: Hill and Wang, 1983.

Bashō, Matsuo. *On Love and Barley: Haiku of Bashō*. Translated by Lucien Stryk. Honolulu: University of Hawaii Press, 1985.

———. *Narrow Road to the Interior*. Translated by Sam Hamill. Boston: Shambhala Publications, Inc., 1998.

Buson, Yosa. *Haiku Master Buson*. Translated by Yuki Sawa and Edith Marcombe Shiffert. San Francisco: Heian International, 1978.

A Collection of Tales from Uji: A Study and Translation of Uji Shūi Monogatari. Translated by D.E. Mills. Cambridge (UK): Cambridge UP, 1970.

Endo, Shusaku. "A Fifty-Year-Old Man." *Five by Endo*. Translated by Van C. Gessel. New York: New Directions, 2000.

Fujino, Chiya. "Her Room." *Inside and Other Short Fiction*. Translated by Cathy Lane. Tokyo: Kodansha International, 2006.

Fukukita, Yasunosuke. *The Tea Cult of Japan*. Tokyo: Japan Travel Bureau, 1955.

Hersey, John. *Hiroshima*. New York: Penguin, 1946.

Honda, Ishiro and Takeo Murata, screenwriters. *Gojira*. Toho Film Company, 1954.

Ibuse, Masuji. *Black Rain*. Translated by John Bester. Tokyo: Kodansha, 1980.

Kamo, Chōmei. "An Account of My Hut." *Anthology of Japanese Literature*. Edited and translated by Donald Keene. New York: Grove Press, 1955.

Katō, Genchi. *A Study of Shintō: The Religion of the Japanese Nation*. Tokyo: Meiji Japan Society, 1926.

Kawabata, Yasunari. *Snow Country*. Translated by Edward G Seidensticker. New York: Vintage, 1996.

Kirino, Natsuo. *Out*. Translated by Stephen Snyder. New York: Vintage, 2003.

Lennon, John. "Oh Yoko!" *Imagine*, Apple Records, 1971.

Mishima, Yukio. "Patriotism." *Death in Midsummer and Other Stories*. Translated by Geoffrey Sargent. New York: New Directions, 1966.

———. *The Way of the Samurai: Yukio Mishima on Hagakure in Modern Life*. Translated by Kathryn Sparling. New York: Basic Books, 1977.

Murakami, Haruki. "Super-Frog Saves Tokyo." *After the Quake*. Translated by Jay Rubin. New York: Vintage, 2002.

———. *Underground: The Tokyo Gas Attack and the Japanese Psyche*. Translated by Alfred Birnbaum & Philip Gabriel. New York: Vintage, 2001.

Nishikawa, Issōtei. *Floral Art of Japan*. Tokyo: Japan Travel Bureau, 1949.

Ooka, Shohei. *Fires on the Plain*. Translated by Ivan Morris. New York: A.A. Knopf, 1957.

Perry, Matthew C. and Francis L. Hawks. *Narrative of the Expedition of an American Squadron to the China Seas and Japan, Performed in the Years 1852, 1853 and 1854 Under the Command of Commodore M.C. Perry, United States Navy*. Washington DC: A.O.P. Nicholson, 1856.

Sankei, Saito. *Kobe Hotel*. Translated by Saito Masaya. Tokyo: Weatherhill, 1993.

Shikibu, Murasaki. *The Tale of Genji*. Translated by Edward G. Seidensticker. New York: Vintage, 1985.

Shōnagon, Sei. *The Pillow Book of Sei Shōnagon*. Translated by Ivan Morris. New York: Columbia UP, 1991.

Takamiyama, Daigorō and John Krepps Wheeler. *Takamiyama: The World of Sumo*. Tokyo: Kodansha, 1973.

Tale of the Heike. Translated by Helen Craig McCullough. Stanford: Stanford UP, 1988.

Tales of Ise. Translated by H. Jay Harris. Tokyo: Charles E. Tuttle Company, 1972.

Tanizaki, Jun'ichirō. "The Gourmet Club." *The Gourmet Club: A Sextet*. Translated by Anthony H. Chambers and Paul McCarthy. Tokyo: Kodansha, 2003.

———. *In Praise of Shadows*. Translated by Thomas J. Harper and Edward G. Seidensticker. New Haven: Leete's Island Books, 1977.

Vollmann, William T. *Into the Forbidden Zone: A Trip Through Hell and High Water in Post-Earthquake Japan*. San Francisco: Byliner Inc., 2011.

Yu, Miri. *Gold Rush*. Translated by Stephen Snyder. New York: Welcome Rain, 2003.

Zeami. *On the Art of the Nō Drama: The Major Treatises of Zeami*. Translated by J. Thomas Rimer and Masakazu Yamazaki. Princeton: Princeton UP, 1984.

ACKNOWLEDGMENTS

The journey of this fish story has been a long one, and the manuscript found friends in many harbors along the way.

Michael Martone, a mentor to me still, has known this book since it was just a fingerling. The University of Alabama was its hatchery, and I'm forever grateful for all the support I received there from Michael, Sandy Huss, Lex Williford, and my fellow students. Thank you and Roll Tide.

A tip of the cap, too, to T.R. Reid and Michael Parfit, whose 1995 *National Geographic* articles on Tsukiji and declining fish stocks generated the waves that got me rolling. Reid's story also introduced me to the work of Theodore C. Bestor. His book *Tsukiji: The Fish Market at the Center of the World* was an invaluable resource.

The Ludwig Vogelstein Foundation and the National Endowment for the Arts provided important encouragement to a young writer and essential funding for my further explorations. Thank you. And thanks to Elinor Lipman for steering me in the right direction and to Rikki Ducornet for reaching out.

Agni published an earlier version of "Report of Ito Sadohara, Head of Tuna, Uokai, Ltd., to the Ministry of Commerce, Regarding Recent Events in the Domestic Fishing Industry" in issue 64. Thanks to Sven Birkerts, Bill Pierce, and Jennifer Stroup for their sensitive editorial feedback, to Bill particularly for responding with his own thoughtful report, and again to all the *Agni* crew for their continuing generous support of my work over the years.

Parts II and III of *TOKYO* contain material from pieces I published in *The Collagist, Rattle, Clackamas Literary Review,* and the anthology *Litscapes: Collected U.S. Writings 2015.* Many thanks to the editors and publishers who graciously served up those dishes: Gabriel Blackwell,

Timothy Green, Trevor Dodge, Caitlin Alvarez, Kass Fleisher, and Joe Amato.

Thanks also to Joel Long at Salt Lake City Art, Michael Lavers at Brigham Young University, and Chris Propst at Western Wyoming Community College for the opportunity to try out some of this work in front of an audience. Thanks to Susan Goslee and Bethany Schultz Hurst at Idaho State University for the same, as well as for providing me a place to hide out and write.

Students and colleagues at Berry College and the University of Utah, knowingly and not, have been valuable sounding boards over the years for the ideas and ambitions that produced this book. Thank you, Joe Thornton, for all your assistance. Thanks to all my colleagues and friends for your support, encouragement, and inspiration—particularly Sandra Meek, Brad Adams, Sarah Egerer, Orgil Adams, and Barry Weller. And thanks especially to Melanie Rae Thon, who knows this book better than anyone. Melanie, *TOKYO* owes so much to your attention and passion. Thanks for your singular insight, your commentary, and our walks.

Thanks to the University of Utah's University Research Committee, which provided funding not only for my travel to Tokyo but also for the six commissioned drawings by YAMAGUCHI Akira that accompany my photographs. Thanks also to Janet Theiss, the Asia Center, and the College of Humanities for additional financial support, and to my colleagues Mamiko Suzuki, Wesley Sasaki-Uemura, and David Roh, who provided helpful advice and feedback.

In Seattle, Bruce Rutledge of Chin Music Press produces beautiful books from and about Japan and introduced me to KAWAKAMI Sumie, whose translations were essential to achieving my vision for *TOKYO*. Thank you, Bruce, and dōmo arigatō gozaimasu, Sumie, for taking on this project with such enthusiasm.

Among the many wonders I experienced in Tokyo was the astonishing friendship of SAKURAI Yuuki, who also translated for me (at a moment's notice), made the dinner arrangements, and was a generous advisor and companion. Thank you so much, Yuuki.

OSADA Miho translated, too, and guided me pleasantly to and through all my encounters with YAMAGUCHI Akira from the moment I showed up, unexpected, at Mizuma Art Gallery. I'm so grateful to have had the opportunity to work with you, Miho-san. Thank you for our continuing friendship.

When I first saw Yamaguchi-san's work, I felt an instant affinity and knew that I needed to get his imagery into this book, as counterpoint and complement to all my imagined Tokyos. Thank you so much for our conversations, Yamaguchi-san, in person and on the page. Dōmo arigatō gozaimasu for your perspective, your humor, and your amazing drawings.

Dan Waterman at the University of Alabama Press has been a great friend to me and to this book. The object would not be this beautiful without his support. Thank you, Dan, and everyone at UAP. Thank you, Lou Robinson and Steve Halle and the crew at Illinois State University's Publications Unit, for making the beautiful object.

Thank you, Lance Olsen and the FC2 Board of Directors for giving this fish a home. Your friendship and feedback provided powerful illumination during our final approach.

Frank Mejia, thank you for dreaming a film version of "Report of Ito Sadohara." Keep talking, Dad, I'm still listening. Thanks to my mother, Mary Jean, and my brother and sister, Kevin and Chris, for your enduring support. My Japan began with you.

Thank you, Napoleon and Atticus, for your unwavering companionship, and for all the inspiration I received on our walks and from your curious and clever behavior.

And thank you and dōmo arigatō, most especially and always, to Mindy—my alphabet, my language.